POTSHOT

D1100116

www.noexit.co.uk

OTHER BOOKS BY ROBERT B. PARKER
PUBLISHED BY NO EXIT PRESS

THE SPENSER NOVELS
Now & Then
Dream Girl/
Hundred Dollar Baby
School Days
Cold Service
Bad Business
Back Story
Widow's Walk
Hugger Mugger
Hush Money
Sudden Mischief
Small Vices

THE JESSE STONE NOVELS
High Profile
Sea Change
Stone Cold
Death in Paradise
Trouble in Paradise
Night Passage

THE SUNNY RANDALL NOVELS
Spare Change
Blue Screen
Melancholy Baby
Shrink Rap
Perish Twice
Family Honor

BASEBALL NOVEL
Double Play

ROBERT B. PARKER

POTSHOT

NO EXIT PRESS

This edition published by No Exit Press in 2009,
P.O.Box 394, Harpenden, Herts, AL5 1XJ
www.noexit.co.uk
First published by No Exit Press in 2001

This is a work of fiction. Names, characters, places, and incidents either are the product of
the author's imagination or are used ficticiously, and any resemblance to actual persons
living or dead, businesses, companies, events, or locales is entirely coincidental.

The right of Robert B. Parker to be identified as the author of this work has been asserted
in accordance with the Copyright, Designs and Patents Act 1988.

A CIP catalogue record for this book is available from the British Library.

ISBN 978-1-84243-326-3

6 8 10 9 7

Printed and bound in Great Britain by CPI Cox & Wyman, Reading, Berks

for joan:
somewhere around the twelfth of never.

POT SHOT

chapter
I

SHE WAS WEARING a straw hat, pulled down over her forehead, a short flowered dress, no stockings and white high heels. A lot of blond hair showed under the hat. Her face was nearly angelic and looked about 15, though the fact that she wore a wedding ring made me skeptical. She marched into my office like someone volunteering for active duty, and sat in one of my client chairs with her feet flat on the floor and her knees together. Nice knees.

"You're Mr. Spenser."

"I am."

"Lieutenant Samuelson of the Los Angeles Police Department said I should talk to you."

"He's right," I said.

"You know about this already?"

"No," I said. "I just think everybody should talk to me."

"Oh, yes . . . My name is Mary Lou Buckman."

"How do you do Mrs. Buckman."

"Fine, thank you."

She was quiet for a moment, as if she wasn't quite sure what she should do next. I didn't know either, so I sat and waited. Her bare legs were tan. Not tan as if she'd slathered them with oil and baked in the sun—tan as if she'd spent time outdoors in shorts. Her eyes were as big as Susan's, and bright blue.

Finally she said, "I would like to hire you."

"Okay."

"Don't you want to know more than that?"

"I wanted to start on a positive note," I said.

"I don't know if you're serious or if you're laughing at me," she said.

"I'm not always sure myself," I said. "What would you like me to do?"

She took a deep breath.

"I live in a small town in the foothills of the Saw Tooth Mountains, called Potshot. Once it was a rendezvous for mountain men, now it's a western retreat for a lot of people, mostly from L.A., with money, who've moved there with the idea of getting their lives back into a more fundamental rhythm."

"Back out of all this now too much for us," I said.

"That's a poem or something," she said.

"Frost," I said.

She nodded.

"My husband and I came from Los Angeles. He was a football coach, Fairfax High. We got sick of the life and moved out here, there actually. We run, ran, a little tourist service, take people on horseback into the mountains and back—nothing fancy, day trips, maybe a picnic lunch."

" 'We *ran* a service'? " I said.

"I still run it. My husband is dead."

She said it as calmly as if I'd asked his name. No effect. I nodded.

"There was always an element to the town," she said. "I suppose you could call it a criminal element—they tended to congregate in the hills above town, a place called the Dell. There's an old mine there that somebody started once, and they never found anything and abandoned it, along with the mine buildings. They are, I suppose, sort of contemporary mountain men, people who made a living from the mountains. You know, fur trapping, hunting, scavenging. I think there are people still looking for gold, or silver, or whatever they think is in there—I don't know anything about mining. Some people have been laid off from the lumber companies, or the strip mines, there's a few left over hippies, and a general assortment of panhandlers and drunks and potheads."

"Which probably interferes with the natural rhythm of it all," I said.

"They were no more bothersome than any fringe people in any place," she said, "until about three years ago."

"What happened three years ago?"

"They got organized," she said. "They became a gang."

"Who organized them?"

"I don't know his real name. He calls himself The Preacher."

"Is he a preacher?"

"I don't know. I think so. I don't think he's being ironic."

"And there's a problem," I said.

"The gang lives off the town. They require the businessmen to pay protection. They use the stores and the restaurants and bars and don't pay. They acquire businesses in town for less than they're worth by driving out the owners. They bully the men. Bother the women."

"Cops?"

"We have a police chief. He's a pleasant man. Very likable. But he does nothing. I don't know if he's been bribed, or if he's afraid or both."

"Sheriff's Department?"

"The sheriff's deputies come out, if they're called." she said. "But it's a long way and when they arrive, there are never any witnesses."

"So why are you telling me all this?"

She shifted in her chair, and pulled the hem of her skirt down as if she could cover her knees, which she couldn't. She didn't seem to be wearing any perfume, but she generated a small scent of expensive soap.

"They killed my husband."

"I'm sorry," I said.

"He was in the Marine Corps. He played football in college," she said. "He was a very courageous man. An entirely wonderful man."

Her voice was flat and without inflection, as if she were reciting something she'd memorized.

"He wouldn't pay the Dell any money," she said. "So they killed him."

"Witnesses?"

"No one has come forward."

"How do you know it was the, ah, Dell?" I said.

"They threatened him, if he didn't pay. Who else would it be?"

"And you want me to find out which one did it?"

"Yes and see that they go to jail."

"Can you pay?"

"Yes. Up to a point."

"We'll come in under the point," I said.

She shifted in her chair again and crossed her legs, and rested her folded hands on her thigh.

"Why didn't you just sell and get out?" I said. "Move to Park City or someplace?"

"There's no market for homes anymore. No one wants to move there because of the Dell gang."

"And you knew Samuelson from your L.A. days."

"His son played for Steve . . . my husband."

"And you asked him about getting some help and he suggested me."

"Yes. He said you were good and you'd keep your word."

"A good description," I said.

"He also said you were too sure of yourself. And not as funny as you thought you were."

"Well he's wrong on the last one," I said. "But no need to argue."

"Will you do it?

"Okay," I said.

"Just like that?"

"Yep."

"What are you going to do?"

"Come out and poke around."

"That's all?"

"It's a start," I said.

chapter
2

P OTSHOT WAS IN A valley in the early stages of ascending
foothills, which became at some indeterminate point the Saw-
tooth Mountains. There were ostentatious homes above the town.
The town was expensive faux western with wooden sidewalks and
places with names like The Rattlesnake Cafe and the Coyote
Grill. There was a three-story hotel that called itself The Jack Rabbit Inn. It had a wide front porch. Inside, the first floor had a registration desk, a restaurant and a bar in the lobby. To the right of
the registration desk there was an open stairway leading up to the
bedrooms. My room was one flight up and my window looked
down on the main drag. The street was nearly empty. A man and
woman wearing cowboy hats over two-hundred-dollar haircuts
crossed the street below my window. They got into a Range
Rover complete with brush gear. The spirit of the old West.

One of Spenser's rules of detection is: Never poke around on an empty stomach. So I unpacked, got my gun, and went down for a club sandwich and a draft beer at the near-empty bar in the lobby. The bartender was a slim guy with a ponytail. He was wearing a western-style shirt, and kept himself busy slicing lemons and putting them in a jar.

"I hear you have some trouble around here," I said.

He stared at me as though I had just told him I was going to shoot myself in the forehead.

"Like what?" he said.

"Like the gang from the Dell," I said.

"I don't know anything about it," he said.

"You know The Preacher?" I said.

"Nope."

"Guy named Steve Buckman got killed awhile back. You know what happened?"

"You a cop or something?"

"Or something," I said.

"I already told Dean all I know—which is nothing."

"Dean?"

"The chief of police."

"So you don't know anything," I said. "Got any guesses?"

"No."

The bartender went back to his lemons. I finished the club sandwich.

"Do you know how to make a vodka gimlet?" I said.

The bartender finished slicing a lemon and looked up at me.

"Sure," he said. "You want one?"

I got up from the bar.

"No," I said. "I just wanted to end the conversation on a positive note."

Outside, the heat was astonishing. I walked past a sporting goods store with fishing rods and nets and waders and tackle boxes in the window. I went in and felt the welcome shock of the air-conditioning. The front of the store was devoted to fishing tackle and hunting knives. In the back it was guns. There was a rack of expensive hunting rifles across the back wall. Along the side wall was an array of shotguns. And in the glass display case under the counter was a collection of big-caliber single-action western-style handguns. There were elaborate tooled leather gunbelts and holsters for sale. And ammunition and self-loading equipment and cleaning kits.

The clerk wore a red plaid shirt with a string tie held by a silver clip. I leaned my forearms on the counter above the handgun display.

"Sell many of these?" I said.

"Some."

"I'm new around here. What do I need to have in order to buy a handgun?"

"Proof of residency," the clerk said. "Like a driver's license."

"Same for the long guns?" I said.

"You bet. Care to look at anything?"

"My driver's license is from another state," I said.

"We can ship anything you buy to a dealer in your area."

"Who buys the handguns?"

The clerk frowned.

"Hell," he said. "I don't know. They got a local driver's license, I sell them a gun. I don't care who they are. Why would I?"

"No reason," I said. "I was just wondering who would want to pack one of these Howitzers."

The clerk shrugged.

"Maybe the guy who killed Steve Buckman," I said.

"He was shot with a nine," the clerk said.

"By whom?"

The clerk shrugged.

"Why you asking me?"

"You're here."

"Yeah, but why are you interested," he said.

"Just a curious guy," I said.

He shook his head as if I were ridiculous, and moved down the counter to another customer. His interest in me had plummeted. I didn't mind. I was used to it. When I left the store the heat was tangible, like walking into a wall. I turned left and strolled the boardwalk. No one was about in the implacable sunshine, except me. *Mad dogs and Englishmen,* I thought.

In all directions but west, the hills rose up from the town in slow, curved slopes until, distantly, they became mountains. It produced the odd effect of simultaneous vastness and enclosure. I felt as far from home as I'd ever been, which was an illusion. California was farther, and Korea was much farther. But the land was so different, so un-Eastern, and, maybe more to the point, Susan wasn't here. She hadn't been in Korea either, but I hadn't known her then, and, while not knowing her made a hole in my existence, I didn't know it at the time.

At the end of the main drag, across the street from a western-wear shop and next to a place called Ringo's Retreat was a small building made of beige bricks with a hip roof and a blue light and a sign outside that said POLICE. I went in.

It was one air-conditioned room. Two cells across the back. A Winchester rifle and a Smith & Wesson pump gun were locked in a cabinet behind a big oak desk with an engraved brass sign on it that said CHIEF. At the desk, wearing a khaki police uniform, was a rangy guy with blond hair and soft blue eyes.

"Good afternoon, sir," he said when I came in.

"Hot," I said.

"Yes. But it's a dry heat," he said.

"The same thing could be said of hell."

He laughed.

"What can I do for you?" he said.

"You the chief?"

"Dean Walker," he said and smiled.

"Spenser," I said. "I'm an investigator from back east."

"Boston," the chief said.

"Betrayed by my accent," I said.

"I can pick Boston out at a hundred yards," he said. "Anyone can."

"I'm trying to find out what happened to a guy named Steve Buckman," I said.

"Stevie," Walker said. "What a shame."

"You knew him."

"Oh, absolutely. Great guy."

"Ever find the shooter?" I said.

"No. Had no evidence. Still don't."

"Any suspects?"

"None."

"I heard he'd been threatened by some people from the Dell."

"I heard that, too," Walker said.

"From?"

"Lou, his wife."

"And?"

"She can't identify the people who made the threats. We even went up to the sheriff's substation in Gilcrest, looked at mug shots. She couldn't find anybody."

"So," I said. "No witnesses. No names. No clues. Just a rumor."

"Exactly," Walker said.

"Case still open?"

"Well, theoretically, but you know the score. Nothing plus nothing equals nothing."

"You have a theory?" I said.

"Stevie was a . . . Stevie thought he was a tough guy. He was pretty aggressive. Maybe he got aggressive with the wrong guy."

"Anything special he might get aggressive about?"

"Nothing I know about," Walker said.

"How about the wife?"

"What about the wife?" Walker said.

"When a married person gets killed, who's the first suspect?" I said.

"Hell, are you accusing your own client?"

"Just asking about standard procedure."

Walker's soft blue eyes got somewhat less soft. But his tone didn't change. Just an open, friendly guy.

"Hey, Spense," he said. "You come all the way out here from Boston to tell me how to do my job?"

"You're the only cop in town?"

"Got four patrolmen," Walker said. "There's a sheriff's substation about forty miles east and if I get in over my head they'll send a deputy out."

"You get in over your head much?"

Walker smiled.

"Hell no. This is a town full of yuppies with too much dough. I feel like I'm showboating if I carry a gun. Was it Mary Lou hired you, or somebody else?"

"How about the Dell?" I said.

Again the eyes changed, but the rest of him was friendly.

"A bunch of overaged hippies," he said. "Don't bother anybody."

"And The Preacher?"

Walker shook his head.

"Don't know him. They all got strange names out there. You know, Moon Dog, Dappa, names like that. And they're probably smoking a little cannabis. But, hey, I start cracking down on people smoking dope, I'll have most of the town in jail. Technically the Dell's not in my jurisdiction, anyway. It's county land."

"So they're not doing anything wrong, and if they are, it's the county's problem."

Walker pointed his finger at me with the thumb cocked, and winked and dropped the thumb.

"There you go," he said.

chapter
3

Mary Lou Buckman lived in a smallish one-story house with white siding, on a cul de sac at the end of a short street on the west edge of Potshot. The yard had no grass. It was sand and stones and several cactus plants. Somehow it managed to look well kept, though I wasn't sure how one kept a stone patch well. Behind the house was a stable and a rail-fenced corral in which several chestnut-colored horses stood in the shade with their heads down, and twitched their skin against the occasional fly willing to endure the heat.

I rang the bell. Mary Lou was in blue shorts and a white tank top when she opened the door. She still smelled of good soap.

"It's you," she said.

"Yes it is," I said.

She stepped aside and let me into the air-conditioned house.

A yellow Lab wearing a red bandanna for a collar jumped up and attempted to lap me into submission. Mary Lou pushed her away.

"This is Jesse," she said. "I do my best, but I can't control her."

"And shouldn't," I said.

I bent down and let Jesse lap me for a bit. Then we all went into Mary Lou's gleaming kitchen. The house was so polished, and swept, and scrubbed, and waxed, and ironed, and starched, that it felt as if I were making a mess just by walking through it. Mary Lou and I sat across from each other at a small bleached oak table. Jesse sat on the floor next to it and looked up with her mouth open and her tongue hanging out. Her tail thumped on the floor.

"This is a dog who's been fed from the table," I said.

"Do you disapprove?"

"No. Dogs are supposed to be fed from the table."

"Do you have a dog?"

"Susan and I share a German shorthair named Pearl," I said.

"That helps," Mary Lou said.

"If you're going to hire a thug, it's better to hire one who likes dogs?"

She smiled.

"Yes, something like that," she said. "Will you have coffee?"

"Sure," I said.

While she was making the coffee, Jesse kept shifting her attention from Mary Lou to me. Food can come from anywhere.

"What have you been up to?" Mary Lou said.

"Well, Mrs. Buckman . . ."

"Please call me Lou."

I nodded.

"Mostly I've been orienting. I talked with the bartender at the hotel. He knew less than Jesse here. I talked with some guy in a gun shop. He knew less than the bartender. I talked with the chief of police."

"Dean Walker," she said. "He's asked me out a couple of times."

"And?"

"And I'm not ready to date yet," she said. "Maybe in awhile."

"He was very interested in who hired me," I said. "He asked a couple of times if it were you."

"What did you say?"

"I ignored the question."

"Everyone will know soon enough," she said. "Who else would it be?"

"Your husband have family?" I said.

"No."

"Could I get a list of the names of people you knew pretty well?" I said. "People I can talk to?"

"Yes, can you wait? I'll have to think."

"Sure."

She got a Bic pen and a white pad with purple lines on it and sat and made a short list of names, pausing now and then to think.

"I'm sure I've left people out," she said. "But these are the ones I can think of."

The list wasn't very long. It was limited to Potshot. There was no one on it from L.A.

"It's a start," I said.

"You won't be . . . ? No. I hired you to investigate. You should just go ahead and do it."

I smiled.

"I won't be mean to them," I said.

Lou looked at me for a time without speaking, patting Jesse's head absently, her coffee sitting in its pretty china cup undrunk. The insistent desert light, cooled, but not dimmed by technology, came in through the kitchen windows and made everything gleam impossibly. The counters and cabinets were bleached oak. The floor and countertops were Mexican tile. The hood over the cookstove was also tiled in the same stuff. The dog's tail moved steadily as Lou stroked her head.

"It took a long time after Steve died for Jesse to realize he wasn't coming home. Every night before supper she'd go and sit at the door and wait."

I didn't say anything. I wasn't sure she was talking to me.

"It was hard to get her to eat for awhile, because Steve was always the one who fed her, and for whatever dog reason, she wanted to wait for him."

I finished my coffee. Lou stopped talking and stared off through the kitchen window at the desert. We looked at each other. She was wearing a light perfume. Her legs were evenly tanned, as well as her arms and face, and probably parts of her I couldn't see. She looked athletic and outdoorsy and clean, and very beautiful. The moment took a long time to pass.

"Not too much is known about dogs," I said.

chapter
4

I STARTED WITH THE first name on Mary Lou's list. J. George Taylor. I was wearing my casual desert detective outfit. Ornate sneakers, jeans, a gray T-shirt hanging out to cover the gun, a blue Brooklyn Dodgers baseball hat and shades. I paused to admire my reflection in the tinted glass door, then went into a real estate office on the main drag, next to the Foot Hills Bank & Trust. The office was a small, round-edged, flat-roofed adobe stand-alone, with a low porch across the front and the overhang of the roof rafters exposed, giving it that authentic Mexican look. There were four small gray metal desks in the room with phones and name plates and swivel chairs, and chairs handily arranged so that customers could rest their checkbooks on the desk as they wrote. In the back of the room was a big oak desk. There were a number of desert-themed prints on the wall: bleached cow skulls, a big cactus, and Native Americans wrapped in colorful blankets, one of whom wore a derby hat with a feather in it. Three of the small inauthentic desks were empty. A woman with a lot of rigid blond hair was sitting at the fourth, talking to a fat guy at the big oak desk. Her makeup was expert and extensive. She was wearing a green top and white pants. Her legs were crossed. Where the fabric pulled tight I noticed that she had a comely, if mature, thigh. Nothing wrong with mature. He had a red face and a lot of male pattern baldness. He reminded me of Friar Tuck. The room felt like a meat locker, but the red-faced guy was sweating lightly. Her nameplate said Bea Taylor. His nameplate said J. George Taylor. Being a trained investigator, I made the connection.

"Hi," she said. "Come in and sit down."

"You want to buy some property," he said with a big smile, "this is the place."

I took out two business cards and handed one to each, and sat down in a convenient customer chair.

"Actually I'm in the market for information," I said.

They looked at my card.

He said, "A private detective?"

She said, "I said to myself when you walked in that door, there's something unusual about that man."

"You're both on the money," I said. "I'm looking into the murder of a man named Steve Buckman."

"Somebody hired you?" J. George said.

"Fortunately, yes," I said. "Can either of you help me at all?"

"Do you have a gun?" the blonde asked.

Somehow she made it sound as if she were asking something intimate.

I smiled at her. The big smile, the kind that would make her mature thighs ripple.

"Are you Mrs. Taylor?" I said.

"Yes, I'm sorry, and this is my husband, George."

J. George nodded like a guy accepting an award. Either he had more stamina than he showed, or she fooled around. I glanced at her again. She had her lips open slightly. She touched the bottom one with the tip of her tongue. Probably both.

"I can't think of anything we could tell you about Steve," Taylor said.

"You knew him," I said.

"Oh sure thing," J. George said. "My business you get to know pretty much everybody in town."

"Our business, dear."

J. George laughed. Jolly.

"Bebe doesn't let you get away with anything," he said.

"I can see that," I said.

Flattering Bebe held promise.

"What kind of a guy was Buckman?"

"Steve was a peach," Bebe said. "Wasn't he, George?"

"A peach of a guy," J. George said. "Organized the kids around here into a Pop Warner league."

"I didn't know the town had enough kids for that," I said.

"Six-man football," J. George said.

"Did you ever play football, Mr. Spenser?" Bebe asked.

"Long time ago, Mrs. Taylor—you know, leather helmets and high-tops."

"What position did you play?"

"Strong safety," I said.

"I'm not surprised," she said, and ran the tip of her tongue along her lower lip.

My guess was she didn't know strong safety from from traffic safety, but she recognized the word strong. I was glad I hadn't played weak side linebacker.

"So Buckman was active in the community," I said, just to be saying something.

Bebe smiled, as if she knew a joke she wasn't sharing.

"Great guy," J. George said. "It's a real tragedy what happened."

"What did happen?" I said.

"Well," J. George said, "you know he got shot."

"Yes."

"Well that's all we know."

"No idea who shot him?"

"No," J. George said quickly, "of course not."

"He have any enemies?" I said.

"No," J. George said. "None. Not that I know of."

"How'd he get along with the Dell?" I said.

"Dell? I'm sure I don't know," J. George said.

"I heard they extort money from town businesses and Steve wouldn't pay."

"I don't know anything about that," J. George said.

He was getting less jolly with every question.

"They ask you to donate?" I said.

"No," J. George said. "Absolutely not."

I looked at Bebe. She was watching the two of us, her mouth ajar, her lower lip tucked slightly under, the tip of her tongue resting on it.

"You know anything about that?" I said to her.

She seemed startled.

"About . . . ?"

"The Dell," I said.

"No. The Dell? No, I don't know anything about that."

"I'm telling you," J. George said. "Steve Buckman didn't have an enemy in the world."

"He had one," I said.

"He did?"

"George," Bebe said. "Somebody shot him."

"Oh, yes, sure thing. I'm starting to slow down, I guess."

Again I saw Bebe smiled at her private joke.

"How was the marriage?" I said.

"Far's I know solid as a rock," J. George said.

He was getting jolly again. Old J. George, fat and jolly. Probably light on his feet. Probably a ton of laughs at rotary club. Probably steal your children in a real estate deal.

"You know about his marriage, Bebe. You're friendly with Lou."

"Lou?" I said.

"Lou Buckman," J. George said. "His wife. Didn't she hire you?"

I smiled. Enigmatic.

"They get along?" I said to Bebe.

"Like George and I," she said.

"That well," I said.

"Oh sure," J. George said. "Been together for, well never mind." He laughed. "Don't want to give our age away. We got married when she was nineteen."

"Wow," I said. "Twenty years."

Bebe smiled almost genuinely.

"How gallant," she said. "Why are you asking about Lou?"

"Just doing the drill," I said. "A spouse dies, the surviving spouse is automatically suspect."

"*Cherchez la femme*," Bebe said, and looked pleased with herself.

"*Oui*," I said.

"You going to be in town long, Mr. Spenser?" J. George said.

"Awhile," I said. "Could you tell me any people that Buckman was close to in town? People I might talk with?"

"Bebe could do that for you. She really knew him better than I did."

I'll bet she did.

"Want to give him a list, Beeb?" J. George said.

"Just so you are, you know, circumspect and . . . I wouldn't want people we know to be pestered."

"I'll try not to pester," I said.

"I don't know why you need this stuff," J. George said. "It was some thug from the Dell, anyway."

"No doubt," I said. "But which one? I'm just looking for information."

Bebe got out a sheet of paper and thought and wrote and thought and wrote. J. George and I sat silently while she wrote, both of us watching her as if it were interesting. When she was through she handed it to me.

"I'm sure it's not everybody," she said. "But it's who I could think of."

"Thank you," I said.

"Anything I can do," she said.

I nodded. The words had an ulterior ring to them, as if they meant more than they seemed to.

"Well anything you need. Bebe and I know pretty much everything goes on around here."

"Except who shot Steve Buckman," I said.

"Except that," J. George said.

He stood. He was taller than I'd thought. Maybe because he

was wearing tan snakeskin cowboy boots. Authentic. I stood and shook hands with him. Bebe stood when I did.

"Sit still, George," she said. "I'll walk him to the door."

She did. When I stepped out onto the covered porch, the heat rammed into me like a physical thing. Bebe stepped out with me.

"Do you get used to the heat?" I said.

"I like heat," she said.

She moistened her lower lip. I could feel one of those comely mature thighs against my own.

"Besides," I said, "it's a dry heat."

"Everyone says that, don't they?"

"Everyone," I said.

"Where are you staying?" she said.

"Jack Rabbit Inn."

She put her hand out. I took it.

"Nice to have met you, Mr. Spenser," she said.

"You too," I said.

"If I think of anything, perhaps I'll call you," she said.

"Anything at all," I said.

She smiled and stared into my eyes.

"Yes," she said.

chapter
5

I COMPARED THE LIST from Lou Buckman with the list from Bebe Taylor. Bebe's list started with a guy named Mark Ratliff. Mary Lou's list didn't name him. Since I assumed he was first on Bebe's list because he was the first one she thought of, he seemed a good choice to visit next.

Ratliff had his office in a corner building with a rounded false front that made it look like a nineteenth-century saloon. There was a glass window to the right of the entry door, in which hung a stained-glass sign that read Tumbleweed Productions. I went in. The reception area was lined with movie posters. The furniture was blond modern and looked very uncomfortable. At the reception desk was a tanned young woman in a lavender pantsuit. Her dark hair was long and straight. There was a dandy silver streak in the front. She wore large, round glasses with gold frames. Her long manicured nails were painted to match her

pantsuit, and she wore an ornate sapphire-and-gold ring on the
index finger of her right hand. The nameplate on the desk said
VICKI.

"May I help you?" she said.

I gave her my card. It was a nice, subdued card. Susan had per-
suaded me not to use one with the picture of me holding a knife
in my teeth.

"I'd like to see Mark Ratliff, please."

Vicki studied my card for a moment.

"Do you have an appointment with Mr. Ratliff?" she said.

"I'm ashamed to say I don't."

I smiled at Vicki even more forcefully than I had at Bebe,
though not the A smile. The A smile was too dangerous. Women
sometimes began to loosen their clothing when I gave them the
A smile.

"What was it concerning, Mr. Spenser?"

"Steve Buckman," I said.

"The man who was . . . ?"

I nodded encouragingly.

"I'll see if Mr. Ratliff is free," she said, and went up a circular
staircase in the back corner of the room and along a balcony and
into an office.

While she was gone, I looked at the movie posters. All of them
had Ratliff's name attached as producer. Some of them had stars
I'd heard of. There was also an article clipped from *Variety* and
framed, in which Ratliff was referred to as "cult film master
Mark Ratliff," which, I think, meant that his films didn't make
money. I was still looking at the posters and listening to the white
noise of the air-conditioning when Vicki came back with good
news.

"Mr. Ratliff will see you," she said as if she were announcing
It's a boy!

"How nice," I said.

"Top of the stairs, turn right," she said.

She smiled at me as if we were co-conspirators. I smiled back.
Pals. One of my best friends in Potshot.

I went up the stairs.

Mark Ratliff was sitting behind a huge, hand-carved, Mexican-
looking desk. He had on a light blue satin sweatsuit. He wore
small gold-rimmed glasses low on his nose. His hair was white
blond and brighter than Bebe's. He was very dark, and the light
coming in through the window behind him illuminated the contrast between his dark skin and his pale hair. He stood when I
came in and looked at me over the glasses.

"Hi," he said. "Mark Ratliff."

The introduction was superfluous. I obviously knew who he
was. But I didn't make a fuss about it. I said hello and sat down.

"So," he said. "Poor Stevie."

"You close to him?" I said.

"My best friend," Ratliff said.

"How about Mrs. Buckman?" I said.

"Oh sure, Lou and I were pals too. But Stevie was the one."

"Any idea who might have wanted to kill him?"

"God, I wish I knew which one," he said.

"Which one of what?" I said.

"Of those bastards in the Dell. Everybody knows it was one
of them."

"He had trouble with someone from the Dell?"

"Sure, haven't you even found that out yet?"

"I'm new in town," I said. "Tell me about it."

He looked at me for a moment.

"You're jerking my chain aren't you, Spense? You know more than you're letting on."

"I'd like to hear your version," I said.

"Compare stories, see if you can catch somebody lying," he said. "I know how that works."

I nodded.

"Well as I understand it, he got into a beef with a couple of guys from the Dell."

"Because?"

"I guess they wanted to extort some money from him. He had that little horseback tour business, you know?"

"And?"

"And Stevie was a tough kid. Played football. Been in the Marines. He told them to take a walk."

"And?"

"And they killed him. Show everybody what might happen if they didn't cooperate with the Dell."

"Do you cooperate?"

"Sure," he said. "Cost of doing business."

"You could move."

"I came out here to get away from the whole L.A. scene," he said. "Agents, managers, lawyers, phonies, backstabbing as a way of life? No thanks."

I thought there might be other options besides L.A., but it wasn't something I cared to argue about.

"You make films, you get used to paying off people," he said. "Happens everywhere."

"Un–huh."

"That's what I do," Ratliff said. "It's my passion. I make the films I want to make and I do it on my terms."

"If the deal is right," I said.

He grinned.

"Hey, Spense, nothing's perfect."

"Can you think of anyone other than the farmers in the Dell who might have had anything against Buckman?"

"Stevie, naw. He was a straight guy. Up front, you knew where he stood."

"People like that sometimes make enemies," I said.

"Steve was a good guy. Everybody liked him."

"Me too," I said. "How about his marriage."

"Man, it was beautiful," Ratliff said. "Soul mates, I'm telling you. It's a goddamned shame."

"So you know it was the Dell, but you don't know who in the Dell?"

"That's it exactly," Ratliff said.

"Anyone but Buckman ever stand up to them?"

"Not that I know about, and certainly not since they killed Stevie."

"The object lesson worked," I said.

"I'm afraid it did," Ratliff said. "You think you can crack this?"

"Sure," I said.

"Well, you know," Ratliff leaned back in his chair and laced his fingers behind his head, "if you do it would make a hell of a story."

"You going to make me a star?" I said.

"I could make a hell of a film out of your story, you pull this off," he said. "You be interested in a small option against a big purchase? I'll be straight with you. It'd be only if you solve this."

"Who plays me?" I said.

Ratliff smiled.

"It's a little early for casting, Spense."

"Yeah but it's crucial," I said.

"Well you could certainly consult on the casting. Probably give a credit. Separate card."

"I'll get back to you," I said.

"Think about it," Ratliff said. "I'm telling you."

chapter
6

I TALKED TO FIVE more people that day and learned a little less from each one. Everybody agreed that it was those bastards in the Dell. Everybody believed that Steve was a prince and Lou was a princess. I was sick of it.

Back in the artificial chill of my hotel room, I put my gun on the bedside table, flopped on the bed with my shoes on, and called Susan. She would be through seeing patients. It was always complicated calling her when I was away. As soon as I heard her voice I felt better, and as soon as I hung up I felt worse. But knowing I could call her again made me feel better. There was nothing definably unusual about her voice. But there were colors in it. Overtones of intelligence, hints of passion, an undercurrent of completeness. It was the voice of a beautiful woman. The voice of someone willing to try anything once.

"What's happening?" she said.

"I've been running around asking questions and seeding the clouds," I said.

"As in making rain?"

"As in letting everyone know I'm looking into Steve Buckman's death."

There was a pause. I imagined her sitting on her couch with her legs tucked up under her, the way she did, and her head tilted a little as she talked into the phone, and Pearl the Wonder Dog sprawled beside her with her head hanging over the edge of the couch cushion.

"You're doing it again," she said.

"What?"

"Pushing," she said. "Pushing until someone pushes back."

"Then I know who I'm pushing," I said.

There was another pause, while she decided not to pursue the issue.

"Have you seen your client?" she said.

"Yep."

"How about this gang up in the woods?"

"Hills actually," I said.

"But that's who we're talking about."

"Yes."

"Have you seen them?"

"Not yet."

"But you will," Susan said.

"But I will."

"Have you talked with the local police?"

"Guy named Walker," I said. "Affable, open, friendly, straightforward. I don't believe anything he says."

"Man's intuition?"

"I've been getting lied to for a lot of years now," I said. "I'm getting good at recognizing it."

"Is she cute?" Susan said.

"Who?"

"Mary Lou Whatsis," Susan said.

I smiled happily in my cold hotel room.

"Very," I said. "I told you that before."

"Is she cuter than *moi*?"

"No one is cuter than *tu*," I said.

She was quiet. So was I. There was nothing awkward in the silence. I knew she was thinking. I waited.

"I don't want you to get hurt," Susan said.

"Me either," I said.

"And I worry when you put yourself out as a lure."

"Me too," I said.

"But you do it anyway."

"Seems like a good idea sometimes," I said.

"Because?"

"Because I don't know what else to do," I said.

"So, in other words, I'm in love with a brave idiot."

"Better than a scared one," I said.

"Sometimes . . ." Susan paused again.

I listened to the soundless distance between us.

"Better than not being in love with one," she said.

"Any idiot in a storm," I said.

"How long are you planning to be out there luring the gang from the woods?"

"Hills. I don't know."

"Why don't you find the murderer quickly, and come home."

"What a very good idea," I said.

"Just a suggestion," Susan said.

"Would you like to swap sexual innuendoes for awhile?" I said.

"Of course," Susan said.

So we did.

chapter
7

I PARKED MY RENTAL Ford at the mouth of a narrow dirt road that struggled through the scrub growth and cacti of the low mountains into a short valley, which, according to the map Mary Lou had given me, was called the Dell. I wasn't high enough up to be any cooler, and the heat pressed in on me as I waded through it up the road. There was no sound except the hum of insects in the scrub. I was wearing sneakers and jeans and a T-shirt. I left the T-shirt hanging out, over my belt, to cover the nine-millimeter Browning I had brought—no sense offending the sensibilities of the folks in the Dell. A half-mile in, the dirt road opened up into a grassless clearing with a main house and several Quonset huts scattered about it, and, a hundred yards up-grade, the opening of a mineshaft that looked like hellmouth in an Elizabethan play. There were a couple of four-wheel-drive vehicles parked near the main house, and several all-terrain scooters, and a herd of motorcycles. The house had a veranda, and on it there were half a dozen men, and women, doing nothing. The men's uniform tended to be motorcycle boots, jeans, T-shirts and black leather vests. The women weren't wearing vests. From a long Quonset came the smell of onions frying. There was a satellite dish on the roof of the house, and I could hear television noise.

"How you all doing today," I said when I was close enough to the veranda.

Everyone stared at me.

"Hot enough for you?" I said.

One of the men, or maybe two, got up and came to the top step. He was maybe six-foot-five, with shoulder-length hair, and he weighed maybe 280.

"Who the hell are you?" he said.

"Spenser. I'm looking for The Preacher."

"No shit," the big man said.

"None," I said.

Men and a few women came out of the other buildings and stood, staring at me. There might have been fifty people. The weight of the Browning on my hip felt mildly reassuring. I would have preferred intensely reassuring.

"What you want to see The Preacher for?" the man said.

"I'm trying to find out what happened to Steve Buckman," I said.

The big man frowned a little, concentrating, then he smiled.

"Steve Buckman," he said. "He got shot dead."

"I'm trying to find out by whom," I said.

A fat guy on the veranda said, "Whom," and everybody laughed.

I smiled. Easygoing. A guy who could take a joke.

"We heard about that," the big man said. "You're the guy."

"I'm the guy," I said.

"Matter of fact," he said, "Preacher wants to talk with you."

"Good."

The big man turned and walked across the veranda and went through the screen door into the house. In a moment he came back with another man half his size, who radiated an interior kinetic ferocity that made size irrelevant.

"You The Preacher?" I said.

The man nodded once. He was slender and pale and hairless. He had no eyebrows and there was no hint of a beard. He wore a black dress shirt buttoned to the neck, black slacks and black sandals with black socks. Consistent. He had very little chin. His mouth was thin and sharp and sort of underslung, like a shark's.

"I'm trying to find out who shot a man named Steven Buckman."

The Preacher nodded again, once.

"Do you know who did it?" I said.

The Preacher stared at me without speaking. I waited.

Finally he said, "You come out here alone?"

His voice was raspy, and so soft I could barely hear him. But it had a discernible chill.

"I did."

"Who hired you to bother us about Buckman?"

"Nobody," I said. "I'm just a nosy guy."

"We could stomp it out of you."

"Some of you would get hurt," I said.

The Preacher smiled, sort of. He probably meant it to be a smile.

"You got a pair of balls," he said softly. "I'll give you that."

"Thank you," I said. "Can we sit somewhere and talk?"

The big man with the long hair said to The Preacher, "Want me to stomp his ass?"

"Not yet, Pony."

We all stood without saying anything. It was like one of those awkward pauses in routine conversations where everyone is frantically thinking of something to say.

"We'll take a walk," The Preacher said.

He came down off the veranda. Pony came right behind him. The Preacher shook his head.

"Just me and him," The Preacher said.

Pony looked a little hurt. But he stayed where he was. The Preacher nodded at me, and we walked around the house. There was a view back there. The land dropped away sharply, almost a cliff, and the town and the desert beyond it stretched out like a Bierstadt painting. There was a wooden bench near the edge of the drop—a wide plank nailed on the top of two tree stumps.

"Sit," The Preacher said.

"Nice view," I said.

"Un huh."

It was a strain listening to The Preacher's barely audible voice.

"You know who shot Steve Buckman?" I said.

"What I know," he whispered, "and what I'll tell you ain't got much to do with each other."

"What do you know about me?" I said.

"Your name's Spenser. You're a private shoo-fly from Boston. Somebody hired you to see who killed Buckman."

"You know a lot," I said.

"I'm supposed to," he said.

"So you have sources in town," I said.

The Preacher was staring out at the view. He had high, narrow shoulders, I noticed. When he sat they sort of hunched up so that seen from below, he'd look like a gargoyle on a medieval tower.

"You let everybody know pretty quick," The Preacher said, "what you was doing here."

I nodded.

"I figure that was on purpose," Preacher said. "I figure you're poking a stick into the hornets' nest. See what comes flying out."

"Un-huh."

"And now you come poking up here."

"Seemed a good place to poke," I said.

"If you don't get stung."

"Exactly," I said.

The Preacher made his dreadful smile face again.

"What I'm wondering about is how she picked you, all the way from Boston. You famous?"

I nodded.

"For my wit and charm," I said.

"So I figure you must be pretty good," The Preacher said.

"There's that," I said.

"I'm pretty good, myself."

"How nice for you," I said.

"And I got forty men with me."

"Even nicer," I said.

"So you're clear on it."

"So who killed Steve Buckman?" I said.

The Preacher croaked an audible version of his smile. It was like hearing a shark laugh.

"You keep after it," The Preacher said.

"Un-huh."

"Would you believe me if I told you it was nobody from the Dell?"

"Not so much that I'd declare it solved and go home," I said.

"I'll tell you anyway."

"Did you threaten him?"

"I authorized it," The Preacher said.

"Because?"

"Because he wouldn't abide by the rules."

"Your rules?"

The Preacher nodded.

"Dell rules," he said. "You can look out there, and you can see that it ain't a huge fuck of a lot. But it's enough, and it belongs to us."

"Like a carcass belongs to vultures?" I said.

The Preacher smiled without showing any teeth. They were probably pointed.

"Except that it ain't dead," he said.

"And Buckman?"

"We charged him rent for his business. He refused to pay it. He was told there would be a penalty."

"That bring him around?" I said.

"No."

"So?"

"So somebody shot him," The Preacher said.

"Not you."

"Not none of us. We was going to stomp his sorry ass. But we'd rather have him alive and earning so he could pay his rent."

"How about his widow?" I said. "I understand she runs the business now."

"We'll get to her," The Preacher said. "We thought we'd let the murder thing sort of burn out, 'fore we hit on her."

"Grieving widow," I said.

"Sure," The Preacher said.

"Sheriff's detectives," I said.

"Sure."

"So that's the local industry here in the Dell?" I said. "Living off the town?"

"We was here first," The Preacher said.

"We was?"

"Been people in the Dell since the Mexican War."

"Your ancestors?" I said.

"What you might call spir-it-u-al ancestors," The Preacher said. "Been people like us living here hundred and sixty years."

"Supporting themselves off the town," I said.

"Hell," The Preacher said, "we was the town at first. Then the mine went dry, and all the fucking yuppies moved in. There's the money. Might as well take it."

"Whether they want to give it or not."

"You think lambs want to get eaten by wolves?" The Preacher said.

"So are you really a preacher?"

"I preach," he said.

"What?"

"What do I preach?"

"Un-huh."

"I preach self-reliance," he said.

He didn't seem to be kidding.

"You and Emerson," I said.

"Who's Emerson?"

"One of the Concord Transcendentalists," I said.

He frowned. I seemed to be serious.

"Are you fucking with me?" The Preacher said.

"Sometimes I can't help myself."

He stared at me like some kind of reptilian predator. I could feel it in the small recesses of my stomach.

"Could get you hurt really bad," he said.

"How long you been here?" I said.

"I come here about three years ago," The Preacher said. "Found a bunch of degenerate bums, no rules, no ambition, fighting each other over booze and dope and women. I put in some rules, turned them into something."

"What rules?"

"No dope. No hard booze. No fighting with each other. No unattached broads. Any women come here, the man that brought them is responsible for them. You fight with one of us, you fight with all of us."

"You gave them pride," I said.

He studied me again. This time, his gaze was no less reptilian, but it wasn't predatory.

"Yeah," he whispered, "you might say so."

"Probably got some for yourself," I said.

He stared out over the desert flats below us, for a time. The heat shimmered up over the town.

"You might be a smart fella," he said after a time.

"I might be," I said.

He looked closely at his fingertips as he rubbed them together. The temperature was ferociously hot. I knew I was sweating. But the sweat evaporated almost instantly in the dry air.

"I come in here," The Preacher said, "these people were lying around here like zoo animals," he said. "Farting, fucking, fighting over the women. Dope, booze. They ran out of money they'd boost something in town, or beg. Nobody cleaned the barracks. Nobody washed themselves. The place stunk."

I nodded.

"You know Buckman?" I said.

"I knew him."

"Know his wife?"

"Enough," The Preacher said.

"You got any thought who shot him?"

"You're like a fucking dog with a fucking bone," The Preacher said. "Maybe she shot him."

"Mrs. Buckman?"

"Could be."

"Got any reason to think so?"

The Preacher laughed his dry, ugly laugh.

"*Cherchez la* fucking *femme*," he said. "Ain't that right?"

Him too.

"Sometimes."

"More than sometimes," The Preacher said. "Broads are trouble."

"I take it you're not a feminist," I said.

"A what?"

"Never mind."

The feral ferocity came back into his look.

"You fucking with me again?" he said.

"Only a little," I said.

"You take some bad chances, Boston."

"Keeps me young," I said.

The Preacher cackled. It was a startling sound.

"Well you go ahead and find out who killed old Stevie Buckman," The Preacher said. "And good luck with it . . . long as you stay out of our way."

"Do what I can," I said.

chapter
8

BACK AT THE Jack Rabbit Inn I went to the bar. I liked air-conditioned bars on hot afternoons, when there weren't many people there and it was quiet and sort of dim. They had Coors on draught. I ordered some and it arrived in a chilled glass. Perfect. When I had drunk half of it, I turned and rested my elbows on the bar and looked around the room. The walls were paneled in bleached oak. There were some Georgia O'Keeffe prints. Behind the bar was a mirror, with the booze stacked in front of it, backlit so it looked enticing. Above the mirror was a large painting of a nude woman with a red silk scarf over her pelvis. I finished the beer and ordered another one. The doors to the bar were bat-winged. Posted on the wall to either side were an assortment of fake wanted posters. The whole look made me want to wear my gun low in a tooled holster. Except the gun was real.

"No one should drink alone," someone said, and Bebe Taylor slid her good-looking butt onto a barstool next to me.

"So I'm volunteering," she said. "Tough dirty work," I said.

"But someone has to do it," Bebe said. "I drink gimlets."

I gestured the bartender down and ordered for her.

"Why aren't you out selling a house?" I said.

"I came down here to see you," she said.

The gimlet arrived, and she picked it up and held it toward the light.

"I think one reason I like these is that they look so nice," she said.

"Any reason's a good one," I said, just to be saying something. "Why did you want to see me?"

"Your nose has been broken," she said.

"Thank you for noticing," I said.

"I like a man whose nose has been broken," she said.

"That's why I had it done."

"And," she said, "I like men who are silly."

"Well, little lady, you've got the right hombre."

She smiled. Each of us drank.

"You know, you're something of a hunk," Bebe said.

A middle-aged couple in shorts and tank tops came in and sat at the end of the bar and ordered vodka and tonics, and something called Alamo burgers.

"What the hell is an Alamo burger?" I said to Bebe.

"A cheeseburger with a chili pepper on it."

"Let the good times roll," I said.

"You're a big one, aren't you," Bebe said.

"Just the right size for my clothes," I said.

Bebe leaned back a little and looked me over as if she might buy me.

"You're not fat at all," she said. "How'd you get so big?"

"Practice," I said.

She reached over and squeezed my bicep.

"Oooo," she said.

"Oo?"

"You must be very strong."

We drank again, which took care of Bebe's gimlet. I nodded to the bartender and he brought her another one.

"Are you in town alone?" she said.

"Yes."

"Is that because you are alone?"

"You mean do I have a person?"

"Yes."

"I do," I said.

"What's her name?"

"Susan," I said.

"You married?"

"Not exactly."

"Not exactly? What does that mean?"

"It means not exactly," I said.

Bebe tasted her new gimlet. Quite a lot of it.

"Leaves you room to maneuver," she said.

I saw no reason to explain Susan and me to Bebe, so I nodded.

"She pretty?"

"No," I said. "She's beautiful."

"Well aren't you gallant?" She put the stress on the last syllable.

"I'm accurate." I stressed the last syllable too.

"Is she as beautiful and as sweet Lou Buckman?" Bebe said.

"Do I hear irony in your voice?" I said.

"Of course not," Bebe said.

She finished her second gimlet in another big swallow. I nodded at the bartender.

"Lou is very beautiful . . . and very sweet."

She looked at her empty glass and looked up at the bartender. She saw that he was putting the finishing touches on her next gimlet, and looked relieved.

"As sweet as you?" I said.

Bebe grinned. She was already a little sloshed.

"Almost," she said.

The bartender put her third gimlet on a napkin in front of her. She picked it up promptly and drank some.

"And how sweet are you?" I said.

"Maybe you'll find out," she said.

"Okay, so how sweet is Lou?"

Bebe giggled.

"Maybe you'll find that out, too. You wouldn't be the first."

"I thought she was blissful in her marriage," I said.

"Sometimes."

Bebe had a little gimlet.

"Tell me about it," I said.

She looked at my half glass of beer.

"You're not staying up with me," she said.

"I started before you," I said.

"You don't like to get drunk?" she said.

"I find it hampers me when I do."

She giggled.

"Wouldn't want you hampered," she said and bumped her knee against mine.

I tried to look seductive.

"Tell me about Lou and Steve."

"Them," she said.

I nodded encouragingly.

"Well I know at least two men she had flings with. I assume they weren't the only two."

"I'll be damned," I said. "Who were they?"

Bebe slugged in some gimlet.

"Who?"

"The men she had flings with," I said.

Spenser, you old gossip.

"Well Mark, for one, and dear old Dean-o for another."

"Mark Ratliff?"

"Un-huh."

"And the cop?"

"Dean Walker," she said.

"And how do you know this?" I said.

Bebe smiled as serenely as she could, being fairly well bagged.

"Men like to kiss and tell," she said.

She might have said, "kissh."

"These guys just stopped by the office one day and told?" I said.

"Not exactly," she said.

"Am I to gather that you were flinging a little yourself?" I said.

She giggled and drank.

"I like to kissh and tell, myself."

"Don't we all?" I said.

She finished her gimlet.

"You got a room?" she said.

"Sure do," I said.

"Let's go see it," she said.

"Let's," I said.

I was trying to leer, but she was too drunk to notice. I signed the tab and took her arm and we went out of the bar and into the lobby and up the stairway to my room.

Inside, she looked around the room.

"So neat," she said. "Whyn't you have room service bring us up a drink? I gotta freshen up a little."

"You bet."

She was in the bathroom for a long time. When she came out I could see that she had worked on her hair a little, and there was a fresh smell of newly sprayed perfume.

"Room service come yet?"

"Not yet," I said.

"Well maybe we should lie on the bed and wait for them," she said.

"That would be swell," I said.

She walked over to the bed, and lay down on it. She smiled at me and patted the bed beside her.

"Come on," she said. "I won't bite."

I sat on the edge of the bed next to her.

"So tell me a little about Steve Buckman," I said.

She stared up at me. Her eyes were unfocused. Her pupils looked very big.

"Steve?"

"Yes, what was he really like?"

She kept looking at me.

"Come on," she said. "Let's do it now."

"You think Steve was different than he seemed?" I said.

Her eyelids drooped. I thought she might be trying to look vampish. Then her eyelids shut. I was saved. She was asleep. I straightened her out a little, put the spread over her, canceled the room service and left.

chapter
9

WHEN I CAME back into the bar, the bartender gave me a
look full of questions he knew he shouldn't ask.

"Beer," I said.

"Will there be a gimlet with that, sir?"

"Couldn't resist, could you?" I said.

He shrugged.

"There's always other jobs," he said.

"Mrs. Taylor is resting," I said.

The bartender smiled.

"She started resting as soon as we got upstairs," I said.

"Never heard it called that," the bartender said.

"Beer," I said.

He brought it and moved back down the bar, smiling to himself. I sipped a little beer.

I missed Susan. I was spending too much time alone in my

head. Solitary speculation is good up to a point. Your mind is uncluttered. You can focus. But with no one to test your perceptions against, things eventually began to circle on themselves. I had spent a lot of time during my life inside my own head. Since I'd been with Susan I had her to help me think, and even when I was away from her, I could sometimes clear my head by explaining things to her in absentia.

It was clear that Bebe was restive in her marriage.

Indeed.

Everything else is less clear. If I believed what she told me, then things are not quite what they had seemed. This not surprising. Almost nothing is quite what it seems. Even The Preacher is a little different than I'd expected.

Of course.

Unless both Bebe and Ratliff are lying, it's pretty sure that Lou Buckman knows Mark Ratliff well, and omitted him from her list. She could have forgotten, though it seems unlikely, especially if she'd slept with him. She could be ashamed of sleeping with him and omitted him in hopes it wouldn't come up. And if she had been sleeping with Dean Walker, it's reasonable that neither would mention it. But it would suggest that Lou also was restive in her marriage.

Cherchez la femme?

Susan too?

Lou being restive in her marriage doesn't mean she killed him. Why would she hire me to find out who killed him if she was the one? Why would she hire me to find out who killed him if she didn't love him enough to be faithful? My imagination shrugged. Maybe she loved him in her fashion and her fashion was different from the ones I endorsed.

Susan shook her head.

You don't cheat on someone you love?

No.

Ratliff was from L.A. Lou and Steve Buckman were from L.A. I wonder where Walker's from? Nobody's from Potshot. Except maybe somebody from the Dell. I've got plenty of time to think about it. Bebe didn't look like she was going to wake up soon, and when she does, I don't want to be in the room. Bebe is a single-minded woman.

Yes.

I drank a little more beer, carefully. In a town where I had annoyed nearly everyone, including the leader of a large gang of vicious thugs, I thought it unwise to get rolling drunk.

Maybe I should confront Lou with the allegations. What does that get me. She'll deny them and I still won't know whether they're true.

Un-huh.

And if she's conning me than I've given away that I know it and my chances of figuring out the con are reduced.

Un-huh.

So maybe pretty soon I should go to L.A. and look into these people a little. And maybe Susan should come with me.

Maybe.

And in the meantime, I got nothing else to do except sit around and see what develops. What if I went up and lay down on the bed with Bebe for awhile.

Maybe not.

chapter
10

I⊤ WAS TOO soon to go back to my room. Bebe would still be there asleep. I wondered if she'd remember anything when she woke up. Maybe she'd think we had in fact done the deed, and would look on me fondly next time we met. I went out and sat in a straight chair on the front porch of The Jack Rabbit Inn with one foot against a post, balancing my chair on its back legs, feeling like Henry Fonda in *My Darling Clementine*. I was alone. A cheery male weather weenie on television had said that the temperature was 108. People in shorts and sunglasses glanced at me in puzzlement as they moved quickly in and out of air-conditioned stores. A lot of them wore big hats. The Potshot police cruiser with two of Dean Walker's four cops in it was idling in front of the hotel.

An old International Harvester Scout with no top came noisily down Main Street past me and rolled to a stop in front of the

store where Lou Buckman ran her excursion business. The
Preacher was sitting in the front seat next to the driver. The patrol car slipped into gear and moved away. There were two guys
in the back seat of the Scout. If any of them noticed me sitting
on the porch like Wyatt Earp, they didn't show it. What's the point
of sitting like Wyatt Earp in 108-degree heat if no one pays any
attention. When the car stopped, one of the guys in the back—
a tall guy with shoulder-length hair, who looked sort of like
Ichabod Crane—swung a leg over the side and jumped out as
agilely as if he didn't look like Ichabod. He went into Lou Buckman's store and came out in a short time holding Lou by the arm.
I let my chair fall forward and stood and walked toward them.
We all reached the topless Scout at the same time.

The Preacher saw me coming and watched me, I think,
through black sunglasses until I reached the car.

"Spenser," he said.

"Preacher."

"Mrs. Buckman been making contributions to the Dell," he
said.

I could barely hear him. The tall guy let go of Lou Buckman
and shifted his ground a little. The second rider was sitting with
one foot on the console between the front seats. He was wearing motorcycle boots, and a knife was stuck in the top of the left
one, which would make him left-handed. He wasn't as tall as I
am, but he was wider, an obvious bodybuilder, wearing a sweaty-
looking orange T-shirt with the sleeves cut off. His head was
shaved. He had prison tattoos on both forearms. The driver was
Mexican, clean-shaven and smooth-looking. They both appeared
bored with the whole scene.

"And she's delinquent?" I said.

"Delinquent," The Preacher said.

He did his soft little snarly laugh.

"That's what she is," he said. "She's fucking de-lin-quent."

"And this is small-claims court?" I said.

The Preacher looked at the men with him.

"Small-claims court," he murmured. "That's a good one, isn't it?"

The other men nodded. I looked at Lou Buckman.

"You want to pay them the money, Lou?"

"I want these men to leave me alone," she said.

I nodded.

"Want to got nothing to do with it," The Preacher said.

I nodded again. Taciturn. Everybody was quiet.

"You're going to interfere," The Preacher mumbled. "Ain't you."

"Yep."

The Preacher jerked his head at Ichabod and Ichabod kicked me in the hip. He would have kicked me in the groin had I not moved my groin out of the way. It made me stagger back a couple of steps, and Ichabod jumped in swinging. He was strong the way some of those tall, bony guys are strong. And he was pretty good. He put out a nice stiff left, which he planned to follow with a right cross. I slipped to the left, which threw him off enough so that I could step inside the right cross and get a handful of his hair. I pulled his head forward and broke his nose with my head. Still holding his hair in one hand, I got my other hand into his crotch and put my shoulder into him and lifted him off the ground and slammed him down on the hood of the truck. He grunted, and went limp. When I stood back, he slowly slid off the hood and lay in the street with his mouth open. I turned to meet the bodybuilder who had scrambled out of the back seat. He had the knife out of his boot top, holding it low in his left hand. He was stronger than Ichabod. And he had a knife. I moved away from him. The Preacher was watching with no expression. The Mexican still looked bored. He started toward me. I had my gun in an ankle holster, but I didn't want to start shooting in the middle of the street if I didn't have to. I took another step back, and slid my belt out of my pant loops. It was a wide leather belt with a big buckle. I had a momentary vision of my pants falling down, and me winning the fight when everyone fell down laughing. I looped it around my left hand so that the buckle end swung loose. Almost gently the body builder made a pass at me with the knife. It was big, like a Bowie knife. I hit him in the wrist just above the knife with the belt buckle and he made kind of a yelp. I swung the belt buckle backhand and hit him in the face with it. He yelped again, and put his right hand up to shield himself and lunged at me with the knife. I jumped back. He came up short, he lunged again and I kicked him in the groin. He was not as alert as I had been. He didn't move his groin behind his hip. He howled this time, and doubled over. I grabbed the knife arm and pulled it toward me and stepped under it and twisted it up behind his back. I gave his shoulder a wrench and the knife fell from his hand and landed dully on the soft asphalt. I shoved him away from me and he staggered and stood bent over with his hands between his thighs, next to Ichabod. I spun away from him, moving to my right, looking for the Mexican. He was still sitting, still bored, except that he was pointing a big revolver with a long barrel at me. I stopped. I didn't see Lou. The Preacher was watching me the way you might watch an unusual lizard. On the sidewalks on both sides of the street, people had stopped to stare.

They stood in little groupings, some of them sheltering behind whatever they could shelter behind, in case things got to flying around. There were faces in the store windows, and down the street I could see Lou walking toward us with Dean Walker.

"Shoot him?" the Mexican said.

The Preacher was silent for a moment.

"Lemme think," he said.

Walker left Lou Buckman on the sidewalk and stepped into the street.

"You're under arrest," he said to me.

The Preacher said, "Walker?"

"I assume these gentlemen wish to press charges," Walker said.

The Mexican rested the long-barreled handgun in his lap, still pointed at me. The Preacher looked at Walker and me. On the street Ichabod was sitting up, and The Bodybuilder had gotten to his knees. The Mexican looked at The Preacher. The Preacher said something I couldn't hear and gestured forward with his chin. The Mexican put the gun down, put the truck in gear, and drove away.

chapter
II

I SAT IN DEAN Walker's cool office with him and Lou Buckman.

"Well," Walker said, "We've given them enough time. I guess they're not going to pursue assault charges."

I said, "Whew!"

"So I guess I can't hold you."

"I don't know why you arrested him anyway," Lou said. "He was just trying to protect me."

Walker nodded.

"That's sort of my job," he said.

"Well isn't it your job to arrest that Preacher?"

"For what?"

"For having Steve killed."

"I got no evidence, Lou."

"Because you're afraid to look for it."

"Or because there isn't any."

"You didn't seem so worried about that when you arrested a man who wasn't doing anything wrong."

"Lou," I said. "He arrested me to keep me from getting shot by The Preacher's driver."

She sat for a moment without doing anything. Then she opened her mouth and closed it again without saying anything.

"That's Spenser's theory," Walker said.

Lou stood up suddenly and stalked from the office. Walker watched her go. She would have slammed the door except that it was on a pneumatic closer and she couldn't. When she was gone and the door had closed, Walker and I looked at each other. Neither of us spoke for a time.

Then Walker said, "You're free to go."

So I went.

I pushed through the heat, back up Main Street, toward my hotel.

chapter
12

THE DAY AFTER I had my first fight with the Dell, I came into the lobby of The Jack Rabbit Inn, and J. George Taylor was standing near the front desk, talking with the bell captain. J. George was one of those guys that would bend whatever ear was closest. J. George spotted me as soon as I entered. I wondered if he was going to challenge me to a duel.

"Spenser. Can I buy you a drink?"

Apparently not.

"Sure," I said.

He clapped the bell captain on the shoulder and led me into the bar. The bartender nodded at me without expression as we went by. In a booth on the back wall of the bar was a round table. Three men were sitting with drinks and a basket of tortilla chips. J. George introduced me as though I were meeting the leaders of the free world.

"This is Roscoe Land, our esteemed mayor. This is Luther Barnes, who serves as city attorney, and this is Henry Brown, who ramrods The Foot Hills Bank and Trust."

I shook hands all around and sat. The cocktail waitress appeared. She was dressed like Dale Evans.

"What are you drinking?" the mayor said to me.

He was a tall, flabby guy with rimless glasses and a gray crew cut that wasn't cut short enough.

"Beer," I said.

"Beer, Margie, and," he made a circular gesture at the table, "and hit the rest of us one more time."

Margie cantered away.

"I gotta tell you," the mayor said. "We liked what you did out there."

"We having a victory celebration?" I said.

"Well," the mayor laughed, though not like he meant it. "You might say so. You are one tough cookie."

"That would be me," I said.

Margie came back with drinks and set them out. While she was at the table nobody spoke. When she left the mayor looked after her.

He said, "That little girl's got a hell of a butt, doesn't she?"

I heard Luther Barnes inhale as though his patience was being tried. He was a young-looking guy with gray hair, and thick eyebrows. His face was one of those pale English-ancestry faces that would never tan. The closest he had gotten was a mild sunburn.

"Could we get to it, Roscoe," he said.

Very businesslike. He'd been to law school, and he wasn't a man to waste time chitchatting.

"Oh throttle it back, Luther," the mayor said. "No reason not to talk a little before you make someone an offer."

Barnes nodded and tightened his mouth and looked at Henry Brown and rolled his eyes.

"The thing is," Brown said, "after what we've seen of you in action, we think you might be able to help us solve a problem."

I waited.

"This is an affluent town, and we have access to a considerable amount of money."

"Isn't that nice," I said.

"It might be nice for you," Brown said. "You know who those people were that you tangled with today."

"I know The Preacher," I said.

"So you know about the Dell?"

"Yes."

"Those men were from the Dell."

"I sort of intuited that," I said. "Years of training."

Brown shifted gears a little.

"You're here looking into Steve Buckman's death."

I smiled helpfully.

"The prevailing theory is that he was killed by the Dell," Brown said. "Because he refused to pay them off."

"I've heard that," I said.

"The Dell is a cancer on this town."

"I've heard, too."

"They intimidate our police. They extort money from our businesses. They frighten the citizens. They come in here, everywhere, and run up a bill and leave without paying. Their presence is destroying our businesses, which depend largely on people coming here for the desert air. Our real estate values are nonexistent. We have complained to the police. They are either afraid or corrupt. I would guess both. In any case, they do nothing. The Sheriff's Department has sent investigators, but witnesses are intimidated, and no one can make a case. And frankly, I'm not sure we are the sheriff's top priority. Many natives look at us as a bunch of yuppie intruders."

"Incredible," I said.

"You're not too talkative, are you," Luther Barnes said.

"I'm a good listener," I said. "And a very good dancer, too."

Barnes frowned.

"Well when you do talk," he said, "must you be a wiseacre?"

"I fight it all the time," I said. "Was there something you wanted me to do for you?"

"We'd like you to rid us of the Dell," Barnes said.

"You mind if I freshen up a bit first?" I said.

"Damn it, this is serious," Barnes said.

"I'll say."

"We don't expect you to do it alone. We are prepared to provide funds for you to hire a band of mercenaries, as many as you need, to clean out the Dell."

"And we sneak in there some night and napalm the place?" I said.

"You do whatever you must," Barnes said.

The rest of the group nodded. The mayor liked the sound of it.

"Whatever you must," the mayor said.

I sat back and looked at my hands resting on the table top. The left one was swollen. If I could get into my room without being sexually assaulted, I could ice it.

"I might be able to help you," I said. "But there are conditions."

"We will not quibble with you over price," Barnes said.

Everyone nodded.

"I'm sure you won't. But be clear about one thing. I am not an assassin. If I sign on for this, I can hire some people, and we can come out here and see what we can do. But it won't include murdering anybody."

"Well how . . . ?" Brown said

"I don't know. My first priority is to find out who killed Steve Buckman. That would not seem to exclude your goal, but you are second on the list. And if we come, you don't get to change your mind in the middle of it and call everything off."

None of them seemed quite sure what to say about that.

"What would it take to make us number one on your list?" Barnes said.

"Nothing."

"If it's a matter of money," Brown said.

"It's not."

"Well," the mayor said, "you'd consult with us."

"Maybe," I said.

"You don't give much, do you," the mayor said.

"Not much," I said.

"Will you do it?" Barnes said.

"If the price is right," I said.

"We'll make it right," Henry Brown said.

I looked at J. George, one of my oldest friends in Potshot, who had sat subserviently through the whole discussion without saying a word.

"What do you think, George."

He smiled as if he'd just accidentally sold a house for cash.

"It'll be great," he said. "Just great."

chapter
13

I WENT INTO MY hotel room very carefully, but Bebe hadn't returned. Maybe romance was dead. My hands were swollen from yesterday's fight. I iced them for awhile, then in the early evening, I went back out to visit Lou Buckman.

Buckman Outfitters was closed. There was a sign on the front door that read I'M AT THE STABLE. The sign was correct. When I drove over there, she was in the corral, washing one of the horses with a hose. I got out of the rental car. Being tough as nails, I did not stagger when I hit the heat.

"Hello," I said.

The horse's lead was tied to a fencepost. He stood placidly, his dark brown coat gleaming, while the water sluiced over him. When I spoke he raised his head and looked at me with thoughtful dark eyes, and then let his head drop again.

"Hi," Lou said.

I sat on the top rail of the fence. I didn't look right. I needed a big hat.

"I talked to The Preacher," I said.

"And punched out two of his men."

"Before that," I said. "I went up to the Dell and talked with him."

"To the Dell?"

"Yep. Preacher says he didn't kill your husband."

"Of course he didn't. He had it done."

"Says he didn't have it done, either," I said.

"Well of course he'd *say* that."

"I think if he'd done it, or had it done, he'd have let me know," I said.

Lou was scornful.

"Because he's so truthful?"

"Because he's so full of himself. He'd want me to know he could do whatever he pleased and get away with it."

"You know him so well, already?"

"I know people like him," I said. "They'd be inclined to let me know they'd done it and challenge me to do anything about it."

"Well, thank God I don't know anyone like that, and I don't believe it for a minute. Steve stood up to them. First they threatened. Steve wouldn't back down. And they killed him."

"We'll see," I said.

"Well who the hell else would it be," she said.

I shrugged. Lou turned the chestnut horse loose and got another one, a darker chestnut. She hooked the shank to the fence rail and sponged him down with soapy water from a bucket.

"Have they frightened you off?" she said. "Or paid you?"

"If they're paying me," I said, "I just recently bit the hand that feeds me."

"I'm sorry, I shouldn't have said that."

"I agree."

She finished sponging the horse and began to rinse him with the hose.

"It's just that everybody lets me down," she said. "I keep hoping and I keep being disappointed."

There was birdsong in the still heat. No whisper of wind. Only the sound of the water running and, now and then, the exhausted buzz of an especially intrepid fly.

"I spend too much time," she said, "thinking about things."

"The mayor and some people have hired me, too," I said.

"To do what?"

"To sanitize the Dell."

"The Dell? You mean run them out?"

"Something like that."

"What about Steve?"

"If you're right, the tasks may be synergistic."

She laughed, though not very warmly.

"Synergistic," she said. "My God! You don't talk like someone who nearly killed two men this afternoon."

"Clean mind, sound body," I said. "I'm going to leave for awhile."

"Leave?"

"Yes, I . . ."

"You're running away. You're afraid that The Preacher will get you for this afternoon."

"I'll be back," I said.

"You won't be back," she said. "I don't even blame you. You can't face down the Dell by yourself."

"No," I said, "I can't. I'm going home to recruit some people." She shook her head.

"I don't believe you," she said.

"Nothing I can do about that," I said.

"I won't pay you any more," she said. "You earned what I've paid you this afternoon. But no more."

"Sure," I said. "While I'm gone, maybe you can count more on the Potshot cops than you think you can."

"About as much," she said, "as I can count on you."

chapter
14

IT WAS MORNING, early. I was drinking coffee with the chief of the Potshot police in an unmarked air-conditioned four-door black Ford Explorer, parked outside the bank on Main Street. There was a rifle and a shotgun on the back seat. Between us in the front seat was the inevitable computer rig.

"When I started with the Middlesex DA's office," I said, "there wasn't a cop in the country would have known what the hell that was."

"Modern crime fighting," Walker said.

"You been a cop before?" I said.

"Yep."

"Where?"

"Someplace else."

"So why'd you end up here?"

"I like it here."

"Sort of hot," I said.

"At least you don't have to shovel it," he said.

"Yeah but it doesn't melt in the spring either."

"You get used to it," Walker said.

"*You* get used to it," I said.

Walker shrugged and drank some coffee.

"I hear that Roscoe and friends hired you," he said.

"You got somebody undercover at the Rotary Club?" I said.

"Small town," Walker said. "I heard they want you to clean up the Dell."

I didn't say anything.

"What about Steve Buckman?"

"I'm still working on that," I said.

"Two jobs at once," he said. "A real Boston rocket."

I shrugged modestly.

"How you planning to go about that?" Walker said.

"If I were going to try and take out The Preacher and his friends, why would I tell you?"

" 'Cause you might need my help?"

"How much of that should I expect if you're in The Preacher's pocket?"

Walker nodded. His khaki uniform shirt was pressed into sharp military creases. He wore big aviator glasses and a big walnut-handled Colt revolver on a tooled leather belt complete with cartridge loops, each loop attractively set off by a big brass cartridge with a copper-coated tip.

"Me telling you I'm not ain't going to convince you," he said.

"No it ain't," I said.

"I do what I can," he said. "I've got four guys, kids really, like the uniform and the chance to carry a piece. Preacher's got forty, none of them kids. I got to obey the law. Preacher can do what he wants. If I'm going to put him in jail, I need witnesses that will testify."

"Frustrating," I said.

Walker shrugged.

"Why not go someplace else?"

"Like I said, I like it here. You going up against the Dell alone?"

"Am I going to have trouble with you?" I said.

Walker drank some more coffee, and looked out through the tinted windshield at the heat shimmers rising from the asphalt.

"I don't want some kind of goddamned range war here," he said.

"Me either," I said. "Am I going to have trouble with you?"

"Not if you're legal," he said. "Maybe I'm not as crooked or scared as you think I am."

"You bought yourself a little credence yesterday," I said.

"Coulda been phony," he said. "Just trying to find out what you're up to."

"Coulda been," I said. "I'm going out of town for awhile. In case you want to keep an eye on Lou Buckman."

He looked very sharply at me, but he didn't say anything. He simply nodded. I didn't say anything either. According to the time and temperature display outside the bank it was 7:27 A.M. and 105 degrees. We finished our coffee in silence, and I got out of the car. I stood for a moment with the door open. There seemed to be something I should say, but I didn't know what it was. Neither did Walker.

Finally I said, "Good luck."

"You too," he said.

chapter
15

IT SEEMED THE better part of valor not to take on the Dell by myself. And since I had smacked two Dellsters around in the public street, it seemed that if I stuck around I might have to. I had my bag packed. I had said my good-byes, such as they were, to Lou Buckman and Dean Walker. It seemed best not to say good-bye to Bebe Taylor. I had my gun unloaded and packed so I could check it through. If the Dell came for me now I'd have to kick them to death.

I checked out of the hotel. Got in my rental car. Turned up the air-conditioning and headed for the airport. For quite awhile I was on a two-lane highway, and everywhere I looked there was only desert. A lot of the landscape was cactus and sage and scrub growth that looked brittle and sharp. It was a landscape in which no horse could gallop. It was a landscape through which a horse would pick his way, slowly, weaving in and out through the hostile vegetation. You just couldn't trust the movies.

After my initial foray, I concluded that all in Potshot was not as it seemed. There was something going on with Lou Buckman that I didn't get. There was a lot going on with Dean Walker I didn't get. And there was something about Potshot that I didn't get. More annoying, I didn't even get what it was I didn't get. It was just a sense that in almost all my dealings with almost everyone I'd talked with, there was another story being told that I couldn't hear.

I sort of trusted The Preacher. He appeared to be a vicious thug and I had no reason to think that he wasn't. It was nice to be able to count on somebody.

I finally reached the interstate and turned on. Another hour to the airport and less than five hours home. There was something exultant about being alone on the highway under the high, hot, empty sky two thousand miles from anything familiar, heading straight for the horizon. And the fact that Susan was eventually beyond that horizon made the feeling tangible as it flickered along the nerve tracks. There were few words in the language better than "going home." Home, of course, was Susan Silverman. It was good that she was in Boston, because I liked it there. But if she moved to Indianapolis, then that would be home. I could make a living. There was crime everywhere.

chapter
16

Susan and I had but recently engaged in some highly inventive home-from-the-hills-is-the-hunter activity, and were now lying together on our backs on top of the covers while the sweat dried on our naked bodies. Pearl the Wonder Dog was curled up at the foot of the bed in a state of mild irritation that she wasn't able to weasel her way in between us.

"So you turned tail and ran," Susan said. "I didn't know you were that sensible."

"The grave's a fine and private place," I said, "but none I think do there embrace."

"Do you mean that you didn't want to get killed," Susan said, "because if you did you couldn't boff me?"

"Exactly," I said.

"Whatever your reasons," Susan said, "I'm glad you're home."

"Me too."

"What are you going to do?"

"About Potshot?"

"Un-huh."

Susan had her head on my shoulder. My arm was around her.

"This is exactly the right moment," I said, "for me to light two cigarettes and hand one to you."

"Makes you regret not smoking for a moment," Susan said.

"Only for a moment," I said.

"So what's going to happen in Potshot?"

"I'll go back out," I said. "Push some more."

"Because you said you would."

"Well, yeah. And because if I don't do what I say I'll do, in a little while I'll be out of business. Because doing what I say I'll do is pretty much what I have to sell."

"I know."

"And, I don't like to get chased away."

"I know."

"Of course," I said, "I could give it up, and stand at stud."

"I wouldn't," Susan said.

"Just a thought," I said.

"Does Mary Lou Whatsis know you've left?"

"Yes."

"Does she know you're coming back?"

"I told her I would. But I'm not sure she believed me."

"The more fool she," Susan said. "Should we get up and prepare a postcoital supper?"

At the foot of the bed Pearl raised her head and looked at us.

"Which word do you think she understands?" I said. "Postcoital? Or supper?"

"She understands everything," Susan said.

"Well she can join us," I said. "Are you ready?"

"Yes."

Neither of us moved.

"Are we going to leap up?" I said.

"Yes," Susan said.

We lay still.

Susan said, "It's time to jump out of this bed."

"Okay."

Neither of us moved.

"You seem to have suceeded primarily in discovering that you don't know what's going on."

"You could say that."

"So why are you home?"

"To show you a good time," I said.

"How sweet," she said. "Is that the only reason?"

"Almost," I said. "I also have to do some recruiting."

"Locally?"

"Some."

"Out of town?"

"Some."

"May I join you?"

"It would be my pleasure," I said.

"I know," Susan said.

She rolled over and put her arms around me and vice versa, and we lay still for a few moments.

"What about your patients?" I said.

"It's August," she said. "Shrinks are closed in August."

"Of course," I said.

"But Pearl could be a problem," she said.

"Lee Farrell will take care of her," I said.

"Will he stay with her at home?"

"Yes."

"Will he try on my clothes while we're gone?"

"He might."

"Are we getting up now?" I said.

"Yes," Susan said. "Here I go."

We lay still.

"I'm hungry," Susan said.

"Me too."

"Lucky we're at your house, not mine," she said.

"Unless we were dying for a bowl of Cheerios," I said.

"I think there's Romaine lettuce, too," Susan said.

Neither of us moved. Susan rubbed her cheek against my chest. Pearl made a grumbling kind of sigh. She might have been snoring. There were no lights on in the room, and the lavender light had faded to black in the evening sky so that it was hard to see Susan. I propped myself up a little with the arm I had around her and turned on the bedside light and looked at her.

"Are you staring at my nude bod?" Susan said.

"I certainly am," I said.

"Jewesses, no matter how seductive and comely, do not like to be seen naked in a bright light."

"I'll squint," I said.

We were quiet for a minute.

"How's it looking?" she said.

"I could tell you better if I weren't squinting."

"Well, just to answer my question, open wide."

I studied her for a moment.

"It appears to be everything a bod should be," I said. "Including naked."

Susan looked a little embarrassed, as if the even the word naked discomfited her.

"I'm cold," she said, and yanked the sheet up over herself. "What's for eats?"

"I could make pasta with clam sauce if I use canned clams," I said.

"That sounds nice."

"I could add peas, if I use frozen ones."

"I'll get up if you will," she said.

I took in a deep breath and slid my arm out from under her shoulders and swung my legs off the bed and stood up. Susan looked at me with only her eyes and forehead showing above the sheet. Then she giggled and pulled the sheet away and flashed me.

"Something to think about," she said, "while you're cooking."

chapter
17

I BEGAN WITH HAWK.

The Harbor Health Club began as a boxer's gym on the waterfront, before the waterfront went upscale. It was owned by Henry Cimoli who had once been a lightweight fighter. Hawk and I used to work out there a long time ago when we were fighters, before we too went upscale. There had been a ring with spit buckets, and heavy bags, and speed bags and an assortment of those little skeeter bags, which I had trouble hitting, and on which Hawk could play Ravel's *Bolero*.

Now the waterfront was chic and the Harbor Health Club was even chic-er. Henry strolled around in white satin sweats, with *Henry* embroidered in gold above the pocket, and asked people if they were having a good workout. The clientele had every imaginable piece of workout gear. Designer sweatbands, wristbands, fingerless leather gloves, brilliant leotards and the absolute latest in high-tech sneakers. Most of the people who came in were so fashionable that they didn't sweat. All the exercise equipment was gleaming with chrome and flashing lights. Ergonomically engineered.

But as a nod, perhaps to his youth, and maybe Hawk's and mine, Henry, in a small side room with a window on the harbor, kept one heavy bag, one speed bag, and one skeeter bag. No ring, no spit buckets.

Hawk wasn't in the boxing room. He was doing dips in the main part of the gym. People looked at him covertly. Hawk would notice this. He noticed everything. But he didn't show that he noticed. He never showed anything, except maybe a slightly pleasant menace.

"I got us a gig out west in the desert," I said.

"That usually means I get no money," Hawk said. "And somebody shoots at me, but I got to travel a long way."

He did the dips very strictly, going way down and back up to full extension slowly. The muscles moved ominously under his dark skin.

"Not this one," I said. "I have a big budget and I'm paying handsomely."

"But somebody still likely to shoot at me," Hawk said.

The dips seemed effortless. His voice showed no strain. But there was a glisten of sweat on his face and arms.

"Well, yeah," I said.

"So what we got to do?"

"Find out who killed a guy. Rescue the town from a big gang of mountain trash."

Henry Cimoli wandered by. He seemed to be bursting, in a small way, out of his form-fitting white health-club suit.

"You guys want to go into the back room," Henry said. "You're scaring my clients."

"Clients?" I said.

"Gyms have customers," Henry said. "Health clubs have clients."

"Health clubs run by little guys dressed like Liberace?" Hawk said, moving his body up and down on the bars.

"I try to maintain a certain image," Henry said.

"You too little to have an image," Hawk said.

"You keep ragging on me," Henry said, "and I'll up your membership fees."

"Henry," I said. "We come here free."

"Well if the Deadly Night Shade here don't watch his mouth it'll be twice that."

"Racial invective," Hawk said.

"Whatever the fuck that is," Henry said.

A middle-aged woman sitting at a chest press machine in pink knit sweats called to Henry. He hustled over.

"Yes, m'am," he said, all smiles. "How can we help you?"

"Is this too much weight?" the woman said.

Henry checked the air-pressure dial.

"How many reps can you do at this resistance?" Henry said.

"Oh, I can do a lot, but I don't want to get big and muscley."

Henry let his glance slide over at us for a moment.

"That weight is fine, m'am. Most women don't bulk up. They don't have the biology for it."

"Really?"

Henry nodded thoughtfully.

"Yes, m'am. Testosterone and all that."

"Really."

"You can use that weight, maybe even add some."

"Thank you," the woman said and began pumping the iron. Henry strolled back over to us.

"How much weight she have on there?" Hawk said.

"Ten pounds," Henry said.

His face remained perfectly blank. Behind us the woman did five reps and stopped and drank from her water bottle and toweled off the machine and moved on.

"Five reps," I said, "with ten pounds. You charge her for this."

"Does her no harm," Henry said.

The woman seemed to be confused by the lat pull setup and Henry hustled over to help her.

"This gang of mountain trash," Hawk said. "How big we talking?"

"Maybe thirty or forty?"

"Well at least be a fair fight," Hawk said. "You invite anybody else?"

"Not yet."

"Good to be first," Hawk said.

chapter
18

Gino Fish did business out of a storefront located in the basement of an old brownstone on Tremont Street in the South End, a couple of blocks from the ballet. The door was down three steps and next to a plateglass window on which was written in black letters DEVELOPMENT ASSOCIATES OF BOSTON.

I went in.

The walls were antique brick, unadorned. At a desk, with dark curly hair and wearing an earring, was a very good-looking young man. He was talking on the phone as I came in. Behind him a maroon velvet curtain separated the back room from the front.

I said, "Hello Stan."

When he looked up and saw me, he put his hand over the mouthpiece and spoke to me.

"Spenser, what a treat, you decide to jump the fence at last?"

"If I was going to, I'd jump it with you, cutie. Is Gino in?"

"Gino's almost always in," Stan said. "Vinnie's with him."

He nodded me toward the back room and went back to his phone conversation, which had something to do with seeing Tina Turner at The Fleet Center.

There were more brick walls in the back room, also unadorned. Gino was in the middle of the room, under a hanging lamp with a Tiffany shade, seated at the round antique table that he used as a desk, reading a brochure for Relais & Chateaux worldwide. Vinnie was to his left, chair tilted against the wall, listening to his Walkman on his headphones.

I said, "Hello Gino."

Gino put a finger into the page he was reading, closed the catalog, and slowly looked up at me. He was bald, slim and leathery.

"Were you flirting with Stanley?" he said.

"Stanley was flirting with me," I said. "I'm in another program."

Vinnie saw me and nodded slightly and kept listening to his earphones.

"And what brings you to me," Gino said.

"I need to borrow Vinnie," I said.

"Really? Where's Hawk?"

"I've recruited him, too."

"For what?"

"I have a job out west that takes six or seven men. I wanted Vinnie to be one of them."

"A shooting job, I assume," Gino said.

He had long fingers, which he laced together and rested his chin on.

"That's why I want Vinnie," I said.

"I didn't imagine you were looking for a dog walker. Have you spoken to Vinnie about this?"

"No. I wanted to clear it with you first."

"Very respectful," Gino said. "And, if I may say so, very unlike you."

I grinned.

"Vinnie wouldn't do it without your say-so, anyway," I said.

Gino nodded.

"Vinnie," he said. "Are you listening to this?"

Vinnie said, "Sure."

"If I can spare you," Gino said, "do you have an interest?"

"Pay?" Vinnie said.

"Good money," I said.

"I'll listen."

I looked at Gino. Gino nodded.

I said, "Let's take a walk."

Gino said, "You don't wish to talk in front of me?"

"True," I said.

"Why?"

"I know Vinnie never says anything to anybody about anything. So I trust him. I know that you will do what suits your best interest. So I don't trust you."

"Be careful how you talk to me," Gino said gently.

"You asked," I said.

Gino nodded and looked at Vinnie and tipped his head toward the door. Vinnie got up and we went out.

Vinnie is shorter than I am and maybe twenty pounds lighter. He's compact and always moved as if he knew exactly what he was doing. Along with a guy in L.A., Vinnie was the best shooter I'd ever seen, and had the quickest hands.

As we walked up Clarendon Street past Hammersley's Bistro and the new ballet building, Vinnie said to me, "You need to be careful about Gino. Just cause's he's queer don't mean he's not tough."

"I know he's tough," I said.

"Gino's okay," Vinnie said.

"Sure," I said.

I told him about Potshot and the Dell and The Preacher. Vinnie didn't interrupt. When I was through he said, "Who else's in it?"

"Hawk," I said.

"And you."

"Yeah."

"I come in, that's three."

"Un-huh."

"Who else you going for?"

"People you don't know."

"Out of town," Vinnie said.

It wasn't a question. He would know anybody in town.

"Yes," I said. "You in?"

"Sure," Vinnie said.

chapter
19

SUSAN AND I were in Atlanta, in Buckhead, at the Ritz-Carlton Hotel. Susan was on the phone with the concierge.

When she hung up, she said, "We have a reservation at The Horseradish Grill at seven."

"Are you planning to have a green salad and a small iced tea?" I said.

"Maybe we could split one," she said.

"I don't know if I should eat that much," I said. "I've got a big day tomorrow."

"How far a drive is it to Lamarr?"

"Couple of hours," I said. "East on Route 20."

"Maybe I'll come with you," she said.

"I thought you wanted to shop Buckhead."

"I think I'd like to go with you."

"On Rodeo Drive," I said, "on Fifth Avenue, and Worth Avenue and North Michigan Avenue, shoppers genuflect at the mere mention of Buckhead. And you, for whom shopping is one of the seven lively arts, you want to take a two-hour drive with me to Lamarr, Georgia?"

"Yes."

"Is it because you are hoping to score me in the back seat of the rental car on the way down?"

"No."

"Well it was a good guess," I said.

"I want to go," she said, "because in a little while I won't have much chance to be with you until you come back from the desert. It's why I wanted come this far with you."

"Because you love me madly?" I said.

"I think so, or it might be pity."

I picked her up in my arms and held her there.

"It's love," I said.

"Yes," she said and kissed me.

We ate fried chicken and mashed potatoes at The Horseradish Grill where Susan flirted with gluttony. After dinner, we drove back along Powers Ferry Road, in the blue evening, as it coiled languidly through a landscape of low hills, high trees and big homes, many of them with white pillars. Susan had her head back against the seat with her eyes closed with the moonlight on her face.

"Post-gluttonous languor?" I said.

"More like contentment," she said. "I've eaten well, I've had some wine. I'm driving through a soft night toward a fine hotel with my honey bun."

"Whom you plan to bang like a drum once we get there?"

"Whom I plan to snuggle until we fall asleep and the after-effects of dining excess fade."

"There's always tomorrow," I said.

She rolled her head toward me and I could see her smile.

"And we're both early risers," she said.

I grinned.

"So to speak," I said.

She smiled and kept her eyes closed and didn't say anything for awhile.

"Are we going to see that gay man you met when you were down here about the horse business?"

"Tedy Sapp," I said. "Gay man doesn't quite cover him."

"I know," Susan said. "It never quite covers anyone."

She was quiet. The road turned. The moonlight shifted so that it slanted in behind her profile. In the pale shine of it, motionless, with her eyes closed, she looked like something carved out of alabaster. Looking at her I felt my throat tighten. I could hear my breathing. Leaving her to go off and rescue Potshot seemed unthinkable. I took in some air, slowly, through my nostrils, and let it out even more slowly.

"We're both wishing you didn't have to go back to Potshot," Susan said.

Susan's eyes were still closed, her profile still ivory. The quiet of the Georgia night muffled the sound of the car.

After awhile I said, "We're wishing we could spend all our time together like this forever, I guess."

She nodded without opening her eyes.

"If we got what we wished for," she said, "it would destroy us."

"Nothing would destroy us," I said.

"No, you're right, nothing would," she said. "But if we were together all the time, it would make moments like this impossible."

"A variation on *Sunday Morning*," I said.

"Not the CBS thing."

"No. The Stevens poem. 'Death is the mother of beauty'?"

"Supply and demand," Susan said. "If everyone lived forever, life would devalue."

"I think so," I said.

"And if we were together all the time, the specialness might wane."

"Or maybe it's all an abstract poetical conceit," I said.

"Maybe," Susan said. "Either way, we do what we do."

"And," I said, "the sun'll come up this morning."

"You and the sun both," she said, and smiled to herself as if she were very pleased at her small joke.

chapter
20

THE SUN HAD in fact risen this morning, and we were a little late getting started to Lamarr. When we got there it was nearly lunchtime.

The Bath House Bar & Grill still had a neon Spuds McKenzie looking raffish in the window. Inside was darker and cooler. The old-fashioned jukebox was the same, and the bar across the back was as it had been, with wine selections and lunch specials listed on a chalkboard. The dance floor to the right of the front door was empty, and there were only a couple of guys at the bar, getting an early start.

Tedy Sapp was drinking coffee at his table to the left. His blond hair was still brightly artificial. He had a new earring, but he was still wearing the Bath House employee costume, green polo shirt and chinos. Unlike the bartender and the two waiters who were setting up for lunch, Tedy filled the green polo shirt to fabric-stretching capacity. The muscles were so prominent, and the body so hard, and the gaze so flat that if I weren't so tough, Tedy Sapp might have scared me. Fortunately I was with Susan.

"Goodness gracious," Tedy said when he saw me. "Ya'll came back."

His voice had a gentle hoarseness, which as he talked, you soon forgot.

"Hello Tedy. This is Susan Silverman."

"The shrink," Sapp said.

"Yes," Susan said.

"And main squeeze," Tedy said.

"And only squeeze," Susan said, and put out her hand and smiled. Tedy didn't appear to scare her.

Tedy smiled back and stood and put out his hand and shook hers. Susan didn't appear to scare him. He gestured us to sit.

"Coffee? Beer? Late breakfast?"

"Coffee," I said.

"Could I get some hot water and lemon?"

Sapp grinned and didn't comment. He gestured one of the waiters over.

"Two coffees," he said. "And a pot of hot water and some lemon."

The waiter nodded and started away.

"And could I have some of those fake sugar thingies?" Susan said.

The waiter paused.

"We have Equal, m'am."

"That'd be great," Susan said.

"High maintenance," Tedy said.

"And well goddamned worth it," Susan said.

"You think?" Sapp said to me.

I nodded vigorously.

"How's the ophthalmologist?" I said.

"High maintenance," Tedy said. He smiled. "And well god-damned worth it," he said.

The waiter brought coffee and hot water with lemon and some little Equal thingies. I put a little cream and sugar in mine. Susan squeezed the lemon into the water, and stirred in a packet of Equal.

"So," Tedy said, looking at the room. "What do you need?"

"There's a town out west, place called Potshot. It's being harassed by a bunch of bad guys, and the cops can't seem to do much."

"They got the wrong cops," Sapp said.

"They do," I said.

Sapp picked his coffee cup up and held it in both hands while he took a sip.

"Lemme guess," he said to Susan. "He's gonna ask me if I want to go out there with him and straighten things out."

"How could you know?" Susan said.

"Gay intuition," Sapp said.

"Of course," Susan said.

Sapp looked at me.

"How many bad guys?" he said.

"Thirty or forty," I said.

"How many guys you got?"

"Counting you, three."

"There's two guys you asked ahead of me?" Sapp said.

"They were closer to home."

Sapp grinned.

"Aside from the fun of going out to West Bum Fuck, excuse me, Susan, in August to shoot it out with forty hoodlums, what's in it for me?"

"You get to work with me again," I said.

"Hot diggity," Sapp said.

"And I'll pay you a lot."

Sapp nodded and drank some more coffee.

"Place closes the month of August so everybody can have vacation."

"What could be more convenient?" I said.

"You planning on hiring anybody else?"

"I have a few more in mind," I said.

Sapp looked at Susan.

He said, "How do you feel about all of this?"

"I wish he were a portrait painter," Susan said, "but then he wouldn't be him, would he?"

"And that would be a bad thing?" Tedy said.

Susan smiled.

"Yes, God help me, that would be a bad thing."

"And you a shrink," Sapp said.

"When you two get through doing Sonny and Cher," I said, "could we sort of focus on the reason I'm here?"

"Which is to recruit me," Sapp said.

"Yes."

"Okay," Sapp said.

"Okay we'll focus? Or okay, you're in?"

"Okay, I'm in," Sapp said. "Though I may have to have Susan talk to Ben."

"The ophthalmologist?" Susan said.

Tedy nodded.

"Him," he said.

"How long have you been together?" Susan said.

"Twelve years."

"Do you think Ben wants you to be different than you are?"

"No," Sapp said and grinned. "I guess he only has eyes for me."

Susan sighed.

chapter
21

I N LATE JULY, in southeastern Nevada, the temperature is 100 and the sun shines every day. No one much cares about this in Las Vegas, because everything is air-conditioned and everyone is inside. Losing money.

I was at the bar in the Mirage, nursing a beer, playing the dollar slots, and waiting for Susan to get rid of fifty dollars playing blackjack. She had brought fifty dollars to gamble with and, since she didn't really know how to play blackjack, it wouldn't take long. I had tried to explain to her that the object was not to spend it, but to try to win more with it. I'm pretty sure she didn't believe me.

Bernard J. Fortunato was across the way with a dark-haired woman in spike heels who would have been taller than he was in her stocking feet. They were playing blackjack. Bernard was looking good in a blue seersucker suit, pink shirt, pink-and-white striped tie and a snap-brim straw hat with a pink hatband. I waited. It was bad form in Vegas to break someone's concentration while he was losing his money. I was in no hurry. I had ten more dollar coins to give to the slots at the bar. Occasionally I would win. But I was undeterred. I would keep feeding coins into the slot until they were gone.

After awhile Bernard J. Fortunato and his tall companion had won enough, or lost enough, I couldn't tell which, and headed for the bar where I sat. He spotted me while he was still halfway across the casino floor. He stopped and stood motionless while he looked at me, trying to remember. Then he came the rest of the way to the bar and stood in front of me.

"Spenser," he said.

I nodded. Bernard looked around.

"Hawk with you?"

"No."

Bernard nodded as if this information confirmed his suspicions. He put a hand on the brunette's arm.

"This is Terry," he said.

Terry smiled and put her hand out. She had on a short flowered summer dress with thin shoulder straps. She was quite beautiful, with big eyes and a wide mouth. All of her that showed, which was considerable, was pretty good. She was carefully made up, and probably somewhat older than she looked.

"Very pleased to meet you," she said.

"And you," I said.

They sat at the bar. Bernard sat beside me and Terry sat beside him.

"Whaddya drinking?" Bernard said.

"I'm all set," I said.

The bartender came down the bar.

"Coupla Mai Tais," Bernard said.

The bartender went away. Bernard looked at me sidelong with his head tilted.

"Whaddya doing here?" he said.

"I'm looking for you," I said.

"Why?"

"Confidential," I said.

The bartender came back with two Mai Tais and set them on the bar on little paper napkins.

Bernard said to Terry, "Take your Mai Tai couple a stools down the bar, while I talk with this guy."

"Sure," Terry said, and picked up her drink and her napkin and moved down to the end of the bar. She didn't seem to mind. When we were alone, Bernard said, "So?"

"Still got that short Colt?"

"Sure."

"Want to make some money?"

"How much?"

"A lot."

"Sure."

"You want to know what you have to do?" I said.

"Let's get right to the amount," Bernard said.

I told him.

"And expenses?" Bernard said.

"Yes."

"Okay," he said. "What do you need done?"

I told him.

"Hawk in on it?" he said.

"Yes."

"Some others?"

"Yes."

"How many?"

"So far, counting you and me, five."

"You got some others guys in mind?"

"I'm working west," I said.

"L.A.?" he said.

"Yes."

"Okay. What's first?"

"First," I said, "is you drive down to Potshot and rent us a house. Talk to a local broker down there, J. George Taylor."

I handed him one of my business cards with Taylor's name and address on the back.

"House should be big enough for six, seven guys. Use any name you want as long as it matches your car registration. Move in. When you got a phone, call me. Don't say anything much to anybody about anything."

Bernard looked at me disgustedly.

"Don't talk? What do I look like, Blabbermouth Barbie? I done this kind a work before."

"Good to hear," I said.

"And I'm a cash-and-carry business. Up front."

I took a checkbook from my inside pocket and wrote out a check and ripped it out and handed it to Bernard. He looked at it to make sure it was done properly, then he folded it and put it in his wallet.

"This clears, I'll head down to Potshot," he said. "I'll let you know."

I stood. Bernard jerked his head at Terry, who smiled and picked up her drink and moved back down the bar beside him.

"Nice to have met you," she said to me.

"You too," I said.

Bernard gestured at the bartender.

"Two more Mai Tais," he said.

I left.

chapter
22

"BUT I DON'T want to stay at nineteen," Susan said. "I want him to hit me."

"But unless he hits you with an ace or a two," I said, "you bust."

"But staying is boring," she said.

"Of course it is," I said.

"You're humoring me."

"Of course I am."

We were in Beverly Hills, walking up Rodeo Drive, the silliest street in America, holding hands, discussing blackjack.

"But what's wrong with my approach," Susan said.

"It guarantees that you'll lose."

"I'm going to lose anyway."

"Very likely," I said. "But the point of the exercise is to try to win."

"I get bored standing there waiting for the proper cards."

I nodded. We were quiet for a little while as we marshaled our arguments.

"Are you thinking sexist things?" Susan said.

"Like 'women, hmmph!'?" I said.

"Like that," she said.

"Not me."

Susan smiled.

We were staying in a hotel at the foot of Rodeo Drive. We liked the hotel. It was expensive, but I'd gotten a supportive advance from the Potshot cabal. And we were right in the heart of Beverly Hills, so we had continuous access to comic relief.

"So much to buy," Susan said, "so little time. How long do you think we'll be here?"

"I need to do a little background on Steven and Mary Lou Buckman," I said.

"I need a new wardrobe," she said. "For fall."

"Didn't you buy a new fall wardrobe last year?"

She gave me a withering look.

"How will you go about checking on the Buckmans?" she said.

"I'll start with Mark Samuelson. He's the one who sent Mary Lou to me."

"Why are you checking on them?"

"Better to know than not know," I said. "Nothing seems quite plumb in Potshot. I want to know about them before they went there. In fact it might help if I knew why they went there."

"To get away?"

"From what?"

"It would probably be good to know that, too," Susan said.

"Hey," I said. "You're detecting. That's man's work."

Susan ignored me, which probably accounts for the longevity of our relationship.

"I have women's work to do," she said. "Why don't you go about your business and let me do it."

Which I did.

chapter 23

MARK SAMUELSON HAD been a lieutenant with a droop-ing moustache and no hair when I last did business with him. Now that I was doing business with him again, he was clean shaven, a captain, and had no hair. He was still wearing his tinted aviator glasses. And he had a healthy outdoor look about him.

His office was in the Parker Center now. It was bigger. It had higher partition walls. And the air-conditioning worked.

"You look the same," he said.

"Yeah," I said, "crying shame isn't it."

"You working with Mary Lou Buckman?"

"Yeah."

"And you want to know what I know about her."

"And her husband," I said.

"My oldest kid played for him at Fairfax High," Samuelson said. "That's how I know him."

Samuelson had his coat off, and his gun was high on his hip on the right side.

"He used to ask me to come talk to the kids a few times, warn them to stay out of trouble. Rah-rah them about physical fitness and staying clean. That kind of crap. Bored the shit out of the kids."

"What kind of coach was he?"

"He was a hard-on," Samuelson said. "He thought he was Vince Lombardi."

"Kids like him?"

"Nobody liked him. Lot of kids quit."

"Yours didn't?"

"No. Ricky's good. He couldn't afford to quit. He was in line for a full ride at San Diego State."

"He get the scholarship?" I said.

"Yeah. Wide receiver."

"Buckman help with that?"

"Buckman didn't help with anything. When the college coaches were around, looking at the kids, Buckman was trying so hard to impress them that he got in the way."

"Looking for an assistant's job?"

"Looking to be head coach, I think."

"Too late now," I said. "He have a temper?"

"Yeah. I don't know how real it was. He was one of those guys who thought he ought to have a temper. Liked people to be scared of him, you know? Watch out for Steve, he's got a temper. He'd been in the Marines. Figured he could chew up a crowbar."

"Was he any good?"

"Oh he could bully the kids okay," Samuelson said. "And he

probably won all the fights in the faculty lounge. But you and me have spent most of our lives with genuine tough guys." Samuelson said. "Buckman was just another Semper Fi asshole."

"How come he left coaching?"

"Got me," Samuelson said. "Ricky graduated three years ago. I lost interest."

"How about the wife?"

"I met her a few times. She was okay as far as I knew."

"They have any trouble at home?"

Samuelson shrugged.

"I'm not their pal," Samuelson said. "When she come in here, told me her husband got clipped in the desert, I wasn't sure who she was."

"You look into it at all?"

Samuelson got up and went to a coffee machine and poured a cup. He looked at me. I shook my head.

"Yeah, a little. Called a guy I know out there, dick in the Sheriff's Department named Cawley Dark. He said the case was dry. Said he probably got whacked by a bunch of local thugs, but there was no evidence and no witnesses and nothing that looked like a lead."

"So you passed her on to me," I said.

"Always looking to help out," Samuelson said.

"You bet," I said.

"She asked me who could help her. I figured you could make something out of nothing, if it got your attention."

"First time I saw you out here, I made nothing out of something," I said.

"You had a bad run. But I liked the way you handled yourself."

"Better than I did," I said.

"I've fucked a few cases myself," Samuelson said.

"People get killed?"

"Once or twice."

I shrugged.

"Where'd she get the money?" I said.

"To pay you?"

"Yeah. Wife of a high school football coach? How much could she have saved up?"

"She's good-looking," Samuelson said. "Maybe she figured there'd be some way to broker a deal."

"It's a thought," I said.

chapter
24

FAIRFAX HIGH SCHOOL is located at the corner of Fairfax and Melrose, not very far from CBS and The Farmer's Market down Fairfax, and excitingly close to the center of black lipstick and body piercing a little further east on Melrose.

The principal looked like a short John Thompson, black, about six-foot-five, and heavy. I introduced myself.

He shook hands. "Arthur Atkins."

He asked to see some ID. I provided some. He read it carefully.

"You are a *private* investigator," he said.

"Yes."

"Well you look like you can handle the job."

"You look like you could provide firm guidance yourself," I said. "To rebellious teenagers."

"We got school police with shotguns. They help me."

"Are sock hops waning in popularity?"

"Waning," Atkins said. "You wanted to talk to me about Steve Buckman?"

"Yes."

"You say he's been killed?"

"Yep."

"How did he die?" Atkins said.

"He was murdered."

"Jesus Christ," Atkins said. "What do you need to know?"

"Anything you can tell me," I said. "I'm just feeling my way around in the dark."

"Aren't we all," Atkins said.

"Was he a good football coach?"

Atkins paused a moment, thought about it, and decided.

"Not for us," he said. "This isn't the NFL. Any coach wants to win. But it's also about the kids. About learning to work hard, and achieve some self-control, and respect one another and win with grace and lose with dignity and cooperate, and follow directions, and think on their feet, and, for crissake, to have some fun."

"Buckman get any of that?"

"Got the win part, though not the grace part. Got the follow directions part, as long as they were his directions."

"Did he leave voluntarily?"

"No. I fired him."

"Any specific reason other than being a jerk?"

"I don't even remember the official reason. There always has to be one. But that was the real reason."

"How'd he take that?"

"He said it was a racial thing. Said he was going to kick my ass."

"Did he?"

"He figured he was a pretty tough guy," Atkins said. "Been in the Marines. Was a running back at Pacific Lutheran."

"And?"

"I been in the Marines and played football."

"Where'd you play?"

"SC."

"Offensive tackle?"

"Very."

"So what happened between you and Buckman?"

"I invited him to the office and offered him the chance to kick my ass."

"He take it?"

Atkins smiled.

"No."

"He have any kind of part-time job?" I said.

"Most teachers do. I think he was a personal trainer."

"At a gym?"

"No. Takeout. He'd come to your home."

"Besides coaching," I said, "did he teach something?"

Atkins smiled.

"Typing," he said.

"Could he type?"

"I don't think so. But we had to do something with him. We don't pay enough to hire a coach just to coach."

"Know anything about the outfitting business he ran in the desert?"

"I think that was mostly the wife," Atkins said.

"How about the wife?"

"Lou," he said. "He met her in college, I think. She was pleasant, perky at social events. I don't really know her."

"She work as well?" I asked.

"I think she worked with the DWP."

"Department of Water and Power?"

"Yep."

"Know what she did?"

"Nope."

"Know any of her friends?"

"No."

"They get along?"

"Don't know."

"Anyone who would know?"

"Woman in our English department," Atkins said. "She was pretty friendly with Buckman."

"What's her name?"

"Sara Hunter," he said. "White girl out of Berkeley. Wants to do good. We're just a tryout for her eventual aim, which is to teach in my old neighborhood."

"South Central?"

"Yep. Work off her upper-middle-class guilt."

"She working it off this summer?"

"Not here," Atkins said. "She lives in Westwood, I think. I'll give you her home address."

He found her card in his Rolodex, and copied her address down on a piece of pink telephone message paper. I tucked it into my shirt pocket.

"You don't know much about them," I said. "Is that typical?"

"There are people on the faculty I spend time with," Atkins said. "And people I don't. I didn't like Buckman. I didn't spend time with him."

Atkins paused and sort of smiled.

"You really are feeling your way along," he said.

"You bet. I just try to keep you talking and see if something comes up."

"Like what?"

"Got no idea," I said. "I just hope I'll know it when I see it. You have any record of where they lived? While they were here?"

"Maybe," Atkins said.

He consulted the Rolodex again.

"You think the Buckmans weren't kosher?"

"I don't know enough to think anything," I said. "I'm trying to find out."

Atkins found the address in the Rolodex, copied it down on another piece of message paper and gave it to me. I put it in my shirt pocket with Sara Hunter. Atkins stood, and put out his hand.

"Good luck," he said.

"Luck is the residue of design," I said.

Atkins looked at me blankly for a minute.

"I'll bet it is," he said.

chapter
25

STEVE BUCKMAN HAD owned a small pink stucco house in Santa Monica, on 16th Street, below Montana. It had a blue front door, a flat roof, and a lemon tree in the front yard.

I rang the front doorbell. Inside a dog barked. I waited. Then a young woman with her dark hair up opened the door a crack. Behind her leg, I could see a dog trying to get a better look at me. I could hear children in the background and a television going.

"I'm looking for Mr. and Mrs. Buckman."

"Excuse the door," she said. "But I don't want the dog to get out."

"Of course," I said. "Are you Mrs. Buckman?"

"Oh God no. I'm Sharon Costin. The Buckmans don't live here anymore."

"Did you know them when they did?" I said.

"Just when we bought the house from them."

"How about some of the other neighbors?" I said. "Would they know the Buckmans, you think?"

"People next door," the woman said. "Why you want to know?"

"I'm from the State Treasurer's Office," I said. "Division of Abandoned Property. We have some money for them."

In the background I could hear some children fighting. One of them started to cry. The dog wasn't a quitter. He kept trying to squeeze by her leg.

"Talk to the people in the next house," she said. "Name's Lewin."

She shut the door.

I said "thank you" politely to the door, and went next door. A woman wearing tennis whites opened the door. She had long, blond hair, good legs and a nice tan.

"I saw you next door," she said. "You selling something?"

I smiled my open, friendly smile. And told my lie about abandoned property.

"Oh, sure, Steve and Lou Buckman. Mary Lou."

"You know them?"

"Knew them. We lived next door for, what? I was pregnant with my first when we moved here, so nine years."

"What can you tell me about them?"

"They moved out east someplace," she said. "Town with a funny name."

"Potshot," I said.

"Yes. That's it. They had some sort of business out there."

"They get along?"

"Well as anybody, I guess. What's that got to do with abandoned property?"

"Nothing," I said with a big sincere smile. "I just heard that he fooled around."

The woman laughed.

"Oh, hell," she said. "They both did. I think my ex may have had a little fling with Lou."

"Lotta that going around," I said. "You know what business they had in Potshot?"

"I don't know. Something to do with camping. You should talk to Nancy Ratliff. She and her ex were pretty tight with the Buckmans."

"Where would I find her?"

"She's still here," the woman said, and nodded at a small white house with blue trim. "Across the street."

"And your ex husband?"

She laughed sourly.

"Mr. Hot Pants," she said. "Don't know. Don't care."

"Thanks," I said.

"I don't want to tell you your job," the woman said, "but if I were you I'd lose that abandoned property story."

I grinned at her.

"It's gotten me this far," I said.

She shrugged. I walked across the street and rang the Ratliff bell and the door opened at once. I had caused a neighborhood alert.

"Mrs. Ratliff?"

"Yes."

"I'm from the Bureau of Abandoned Property."

I was glad the blonde across the street couldn't hear me.

"What the hell is that," Mrs. Ratliff said. She was petite, with thick black hair and sharp features.

"State Treasurer's Office," I said. "We have some money for Mr. and Mrs. Buckman."

"Lucky them," the woman said. "You want to come in?"

"Thank you," I said.

I sometimes wished I wore a hat so when I went into a woman's house I could impress them by taking it off in a gentlemanly way. I settled for removing my sunglasses.

The front door opened immediately to her living room, which was done in Indian rugs and hand-hewn furniture that was too big for the room. There was a little gray stone fireplace with gas jets on the end wall. There was a pitcher of martinis on the glass-topped coffee table that took up too much of the room.

"I'm having a cocktail," she said. "Would you care to join me?"

It was 3:30.

"Sure," I said.

She went through an archway to the small dining room and came back with a martini glass in which there were two olives. She poured me a martini.

"Stirred, not shaken," she said.

I smiled. She picked up her glass and gestured toward me with it.

"Chink, chink," she said.

I touched her glass with mine and we each took a drink. The martini was dreadful. Not cold enough and far too much vermouth.

"So," Nancy Ratliff said. "What can I do for you?"

"Tell me about Steven and Mary Lou Buckman."

"Well, she was a bitch. Still is I'm sure."

"How so?" I said.

Nancy Ratliff took another drink. She didn't appear to know

that the martini was dreadful. Or maybe she knew and didn't care.

"Well, for one thing she was fucking my husband."

"How nice for them," I said.

"Yeah, well, not so nice for me."

"How did Mr. Buckman feel about it?"

"He didn't say."

She drank again and stared into her glass.

"Well, actually he did," she said. "He said we should get even with them."

"Tit for tat," I said just to be saying something, though in the context, the choice of words was unfortunate.

We were silent while she looked into her martini glass.

Finally she said, "Aren't you going to ask me if we did?"

"Only if you want to tell me, Mrs. Ratliff."

"Nancy," she said. "And yeah, I want to tell you."

I smiled happily. She didn't say anything. I waited. She poured herself some more bad martini from the pitcher where the melting ice would have diluted it by now. She took another sip and held her glass up and looked through it.

"I like how clear it looks," she said.

I nodded helpfully. Friendly guy from the Treasurer's office. Eager to please. Eager to listen.

"Yes, we got got even," she said. "In goddamned spades."

"And how did Mr. Ratliff feel about that?" I said.

I had no idea where I was going. Except that Ratliff was a name I'd heard before.

"He left me and went chasing after her."

"And Mr. Buckman?"

"He went too."

"With his wife?" I said.

"I don't know. I guess so. Maybe they were all doing it. A traveling gangbang."

She looked at my glass.

"You're not drinking," she said.

"I'm savoring it slowly," I said. "What is your husband's first name?"

"Ex-husband. I divorced him. The bastard didn't even show up to contest the divorce. I took him for everything he had, except he didn't have anything."

She drank again.

"Movie producer," she snorted. "Sure."

"And his first name?"

"Mark."

I felt very still for a moment inside and then I took a stab at something.

"You happen to know anyone named Dean Walker?" I said.

"The cop? Yeah, used to live three houses up toward Montana. Moved away eight, nine years ago."

"He a friend of the Buckmans?"

"I guess, yeah, he'd be at parties sometimes. Him and his wife."

"You remember her name?"

"Judy, I think."

"He have anything to do with Mrs. Buckman?"

"Dean? I don't know. She'd have been willing. She was like a bitch in heat. But Dean seemed sort of straightforward. If he was fucking her, I don't know about it."

Each time she said *fucking* she said it with relish. As if she liked to say it, as if it were a counterirritant. Like scratching an old itch. Forgive and forget didn't seem to work for her.

chapter
26

SARA HUNTER LIVED in a faux Tudor three-unit condo in Westwood, a block below Wilshire. She was L.A. serious, which meant a loose-fitting, ankle-length flowered dress, some Native-American jewelry and dark leather sandals. Her blond hair was done in a single long braid that reached nearly to her waist. She wore no makeup and despite her best efforts, she was pretty good-looking.

When she opened the door she kept the chain bolt on. I gave her my card. I introduced myself. I explained what I wanted, and I smiled at her. None of it seemed to make her more welcoming.

"Why do you want to talk to me about Steve Buckman?" she said. "He's just somebody I knew at work."

"Well, that's why," I said. "I was hoping for some of your insights."

She liked *insights*.

"Why do you want that?" she said.

There was never a good way to say it. I'd learned over the years to just say it. Which I did.

"Steve's been murdered."

She looked at me as if I had commented on the dandiness of the weather.

"What?"

"We could talk out here on the porch," I said, "if you'd feel more secure."

She didn't speak for a moment, then she closed the door, un-chained it, opened it again and stepped out. She was careful to pull the door shut behind her. The porch extended along the front of her condo to form a little veranda and we sat on some wicker chairs out there. Across the street a couple of Mexicans were trimming a hedge, and on the sidewalk below the veranda, a shapeless middle-aged woman with bright red hair was walking a small, ugly, possum-y looking dog on a retractable leash.

"Tell me about Steve," I said.

She leaned forward a little, resting her elbows on her thighs, and put her face into her hands.

I waited. She sat. Maybe overreaction was endemic. Or maybe she was a very dramatic person. Or maybe Steve was more than someone she knew at work.

After awhile I said, "How you doing?"

Without taking her face from her hands, she shook her head.

"Take your time," I said.

The lady walking her possum turned the corner at Wilshire and disappeared. One of the gardeners across the street was edging the grass now, with a noisy power trimmer.

"Did he suffer much?" Sara said finally.

"He was probably dead before he knew he'd been shot," I said.

I didn't know that, but I saw no reason not to say it.

"Did she do it?" Sara said.

She was still in her position of official mourning and as she talked she rocked a little, forward and back.

"She?" I said.

"Mary Lou. Did she kill him?"

"I don't know. You think?"

She raised her head.

"I think that she would do anything."

"Really?" I said.

"You wouldn't see it. You're a man."

"And you're a woman," I said.

"What?"

"Just trying to hold up my end of the conversation," I said.

"Well you wouldn't. She'd fool you. Blue eyes. Cute. Sweet. She'd show you her dimples and ask for your help and you'd be falling over yourself like some big puppy."

"Woof," I said.

"You can laugh at me if you want to," Sara said, a little pouty. "But it's true."

"Probably is," I said. "Why do you think she might have killed him?"

"Because she couldn't control him, though she never stopped trying. She resented authenticity. She was frightened of the untamed self."

The sky was cloudless. It was 75 and bright. I could smell olive trees.

"His?" I said.

"His, her own . . ." Sara made a you-know-what-I-mean gesture and her voice trailed off.

"How untamed was that?" I said.

"As untamed as yours . . . or mine."

"That untamed?" I said.

"You're laughing at me again."

"That was just a quizzical smile," I said "You know this, how?"

"We were . . . friends."

"Not just someone you knew at work."

"I'm sorry," she said. "That was reflexive. I've become used to evasion."

"The world is too much with us, lately."

"My God, a literate detective?"

"Goes with good-looking," I said. "You and Steve were close friends."

"Yes."

"Do you know if he had any source of income other than Fairfax High?"

"Well they ran that camping business out in the desert. She did, really."

"Anything else?"

"No. Why do you ask?"

"Well Mary Lou is paying me a fair sum to investigate," I said. "Without complaint. Life insurance?"

"I suppose so, but I can't imagine that it was huge . . . a teacher's salary. She's paying you?"

I nodded.

"Did Mary Lou know you and Steve were good friends?"

"I don't know what she knew. She was no trembling virgin herself."

"Mary Lou?"

"See, you're shocked aren't you? Any woman could see through her."

"Why that untamed vixen," I said.

"It was all right for her, but not for Steve."

"Gee that doesn't sound fair," I said.

"No," she said, pouty again. "It wasn't."

The landscaper finished his power trimming and the sudden quiet was almost intrusive. Then as my ears adjusted I could hear the traffic on Wilshire. I kept at Sara for as long as I could stand to, but I had learned what I was going to learn from her and I finally said good-bye and went back to Beverly Hills.

chapter
27

THE HOTEL ROOM was awash with tissue paper and shopping bags. Amid it all, and somehow above it, Susan was trying on some new duds, and examining them carefully in the mirror.

"Would you have any interest in exploring my authentic untamed self?" I said.

"Your what?"

"My untamed self," I said.

"God, if I haven't encountered it yet, I don't think I want to."

"You got something against authenticity?" I said.

"No. I'm just afraid I'll get hurt."

"Maybe later when I've calmed down," I said.

"Maybe," Susan said. "What brought on this sudden attack of authenticity?"

I told her about Sara.

"We assume Sara was having an affair with Steve Buckman?" Susan said.

"Yes. But a fully authentic one," I said.

"What would an inauthentic affair be?" Susan said.

"One which used a battery-powered device?"

"Do you like this skirt?" Susan said.

"I'm not sure," I said. "Better take it off and put it on again."

"Is lechery authentic?" Susan said.

"You bet," I said.

Susan put on a blouse.

"So if we are to believe What'shername . . ."

"Sara."

"If we are to believe Sara, then both Steve and Mary Lou were fooling around with other people, and at least from Whosis's perspective . . ."

"Sara," I said.

"From Sara's perspective Mary Lou was, and perhaps is, a bitch."

"Sara's perspective may be somewhat skewed," I said, "by her being a nitwit."

Susan examined in the mirror the way some new pants fit her. She smiled. Apparently she was pleased. Me too.

"That skews a lot of perspectives," she said.

"Present company excluded," I said. "You wanna eat?"

"Let's go someplace I can wear my new clothes," she said.

There was always something in her eyes that suggested we'd have more fun than we could imagine, whatever we did.

"Does this mean I have to cancel the reservation at Fat Burger?"

She said that it did. She also declined Pink's for a chili dog and we ended up at The Buffalo Club on a dark stretch of Olympic, in Santa Monica. We sat together on the same side of the booth and had a Ketel One martini, or two, and studied the menu. We ordered some oyster shooters and pot roast and ate them. That is, I ate them. Susan had two shooters, and half her pot roast, cutting the other half away before she started and carefully putting one half on her butter plate lest, God forbid, she should eat it by mistake and balloon to 130. I helped. I had her leftover oyster shooters, and the pot roast from her butter plate, and virtuously declined dessert.

Outside I gave the ticket to the valet and held Susan's hand while we watched the desultory traffic plod by in the dark. A silver Lexus pulled up and two men got out. The valet went forward and the first man shook his head. He looked like a mature surfer. Long blond hair, pale blue eyes, sun-darkened skin, which didn't fully conceal the broken veins of a boozer on his cheeks. He was wearing a pair of brown slacks, a brown shirt buttoned to the neck, a small diamond stud in his right earlobe and a camel-hair jacket. The jacket was unbuttoned. The guy with him was all edges and angles. Small, lean, hard, pale, with spiky hair and a sharp hooked nose. His eyes were like the windows in an empty house. He had on big shorts and a flowered shirt that hung over his belt. The surfer stopped in front of me. He stood very close.

"How you doing tonight?" he said.

I nodded slightly. I'd seen these guys before. Maybe not these particular ones, but enough guys just like them so that I was pretty sure what they were. I could feel Susan stiffen slightly beside me. The small guy in the flowered shirt moved a little to my left, balancing off the surfer, who was a little to my right. The valets apparently knew these guys too. They had disappeared.

"You Spenser?"

I hooded my eyes and spoke through my teeth.

"Who wants to know?" I said.

Beside me Susan made a sound that was a little like a snort, but more elegant.

"She thinks I lack originality," I said to the surfer.

"Very funny," the surfer said. "You think that's very funny, Tino?"

"I think this guy could get very dead," the little sharp guy said in a flat voice.

"Life on the edge," I said. "You guys want something or is this a cabaret act?"

"We want to know your interest in the Buckmans."

"Why?"

"Why? Fuck why. Answer what I ask you or we'll mess you up bad. The broad too."

I looked at Susan.

"Broad?" I said.

The surfer was right up against me, which was a mistake. Still looking at Susan, I put my knee hard into the surfer's groin. He gasped and doubled over and I shoved him back into Tino. Tino almost fell, but he didn't. He steadied himself and sort of shucked the surfer off of him, and put his hand toward his hip.

"No," I said.

I had my gun out and steady on his navel. He stopped, his hand half under his flowered shirt. The surfer was squatting on the ground, holding his crotch and rocking gently. I could hear him breathing in gasps. Beside me, Susan's breath was moving in and out a little more quickly than normal. But I'd heard it move faster.

"Turn around," I said.

Tino turned. I stepped forward and took the handgun off his hip and dropped it into the side pocket of my J. Press blue blazer. It felt heavy in there. I didn't want the jacket to sag, but it was one of the hazards of crime fighting.

"Get the blond bomber on his feet and into your car and out of my sight," I said to Tino. "Nothing fancy. I would be pleased to shoot you and watch you die."

Tino didn't look scared. But he didn't look stupid either. He helped the surfer to his feet and into the car that still stood, valet-less, at the curb. He gave me a very sharp look as he went around to get in on the driver's side.

"This ain't over," he said.

"It is for the moment," I said.

Tino got in, slammed the door, put the car in gear, and floored it away from the curb, leaving the smell of burnt rubber to linger after the car was gone. I put my gun away. We looked at each other.

"You do know how to show a girl a good time," Susan said.

"I do," I said.

The valet drove up and parked my car at the curb. He got out and held the door for Susan. A second valet hustled up and held the door for me. I gave him a ten-spot and got in the car.

"Have a nice night," the valet said.

"You too," I said.

And we drove off.

chapter
28

SUSAN AND I didn't talk much on the way back to Beverly Hills. But when we went to bed we made love with unusual intensity. There's a positive side to everything.

In the morning after breakfast, Susan went to the health club and I went down to the Parker Center, where Samuelson introduced me to an ID technician who showed me mug shots for maybe four hours. I never found Tino, but I found the surfer. His name was Jerome Jefferson and he'd been arrested six times for assault. One conviction. No time. They gave me his last address, which was three years old. I pocketed it for later.

"Never heard of him," Samuelson said when I went back to his office, "which means only that he hasn't done anything bad enough to get our attention."

"Or you haven't caught him at it," I said.

Samuelson shrugged.

"Six assaults? Whatever he is, he's a gofer," Samuelson said.

"How about OCU?" I said. "This wasn't his own idea. Somebody sent him."

"I'll call over there," Samuelson said. "Sheriff's department, too."

"If they don't know Jefferson," I said, "try Tino. My guess is that Jefferson's the slugger and Tino's the shooter."

"Or at least that's the way it was supposed to work out."

"The way it was supposed to work out, I was supposed to get faint with fear and go right home," I said. "And never make audible mention of Steve or Mary Lou Buckman again."

"Audible mention," Samuelson said.

"I'm sleeping with a Ph.D.," I said.

"You might want to talk to your friend del Rio again," Samuelson said.

"Again?" I said. "You're keeping track of me?"

"We're keeping track of del Rio," Samuelson said.

"He's not exactly my friend," I said.

"Well he must like you. If he didn't, I'd be looking into your death."

"Or his," I said.

Back in my rental car, I picked up Sunset down from the Civic Center, turned up the air-conditioning, and headed west. Jerome Jefferson's last known residence was a three-story white stucco apartment building on Las Palmas just below Fountain. It had the sort of slick, sleazy look that only Los Angeles has fully mastered, with tiny useless balconies of green iron outside the windows.

There was no listing for Jerome Jefferson at the entry. I rang the bell marked SUPER. And after my third ring, he woke up from his nap and slouched to the door in his slippers. He was wearing an old-fashioned undershirt and plaid knee-length shorts. He had a two-day stubble, mostly gray. His long, limp hair was mostly gray, and showed no sign of shower or shampoo.

"No vacancy," he said.

"I don't see why," I said.

"Huh?"

"Implied criticism," I said. "I'm looking for a guy named Jerome Jefferson. Big guy, blond hair. Looks like a boozer."

"He ain't here," the Super said, "and he ain't coming back. The management company evicted him."

"Rent?"

"Yeah. Fucker never paid. Company kept telling me to talk with him. You know him?"

"I've met him," I said.

"Then you know what'd be like to try and talk with him. They don't pay me enough for me to get my teeth kicked in."

"You know where he went?" I said.

"Heard he moved in with some broad he was scoring in West Hollywood."

"Address?"

"Got no idea," the super said. "Maybe they know at the company, they been trying to get the rent he owes them."

There was a sign beside the entry that read MANAGED BY SOUTHLAND PROPERTIES, with an address in Century City.

"You know his friend?" I said. "Smaller guy. Thin. Big, sharp beak."

The super shook his head.

"I hope you find the bastard. You look like you might give him trouble."

"I might," I said.

"You got the build for it anyway."

"Thanks for the encouragement," I said.

He nodded blankly and closed the door and shuffled off back to his nap.

Century City is a cluster of expensive high-rises just below the Los Angeles Country Club that occupies a former movie back-lot between Santa Monica and Olympic. There was a big hotel there, and a shopping mall and a theater and a supermarket and the offices of anyone on the west side that wanted a good address. Southland Properties was on the fifteenth floor of a building on Constellation Avenue, with a nice view of the Century Plaza Hotel. I was passed along the chain of command at Southland until I was in the office of their financial compliance manager, whose name, according to the nameplate on his desk, was Karl Adams.

We shook hands and he gestured me to a seat.

"Karl Adams," he said. "You're looking for Jerome Jefferson."

Adams was about my height, and lean. He looked like retired military.

"I am," I said.

"We are too," Adams said. "He owes us six months' rent. What's your interest?"

"I'm trying to see what his connection is to a case I'm working on."

My card was lying on Adams's desk. He glanced down at it.

"In Boston?" he said.

"Town called Potshot," I said. "In the desert."

"Long way from home," Adams said.

"Anywhere I hang my hat."

"Yeah sure," he said.

He paused and was thoughtful for a small time. Then he said, "Don't see why not."

"Me either."

"I'll tell you what I know," Adams said. "And if you were to find him, I'd appreciate a jingle."

"Seems fair to me," I said.

"After he skipped out of the place on Las Palmas, we figure he moved in with his girlfriend on Franklin Avenue. So we went up there but she says she's broken up with him and hasn't seen him and never wants to see him again."

"You believe her?"

"No. So we put somebody up there for a couple days but there was no sign of him."

"Round the clock?" I said.

"Hell no. We don't have the manpower for real surveillance."

"So if he didn't come and go between nine and five you wouldn't know if he was there."

"Correct."

"You got much experience skip tracing?"

"Financial compliance," Adams said. "Says so on my door."

"Sure," I said.

"I'm retired Navy," Adams said. "Intelligence. I got a lower budget here."

"You got a name and address for the girlfriend?" I said.

"Yeah."

He took one of his business cards out of a small container on his desk and wrote on the back.

"Here you go," he said. "You need directions?"

"No," I said. "I've screwed up cases out here before."

chapter
29

THE GIRLFRIEND'S NAME was Carlotta Hopewell. She had a small clapboard house with an overhanging roof on the front porch. The house was in Hollywood, where it crouched among the apartment buildings on Franklin Street between Gower and Vine. The yard needed work, and some of the white paint was peeling from the clapboards. As I walked up the front walk, a woman who must have been watching out the window opened the door and stepped out onto the front steps. She had a glass of white wine in her hand and she smelled strongly of it.

"May I help you?" she said.

Her lips were pouty and her face was puffy. She had loud blond hair and not much muscle tone. She was wearing shorts and a short tank top that stopped several inches above above her navel. Her body was pale and soft-looking.

"Carlotta Hopewell?"

"Yes?"

"I'm looking for a man named Jerome Jefferson."

"I'm not him."

"Good," I said. "That's helpful. It narrows the search."

"Hey you're kind of funny, huh?"

"But I have a serious side. Is Jerome staying with you?"

"Naw."

She swirled her wine a little.

"But you know him," I said.

"Maybe. You want some wine?"

"Yes, thank you," I said.

She opened the screen door and we went in. Ah, memories of things past. There was a rough woven orange rug on the floor of her living room, and a huge picture of Prince covering most of the wall above a brown suede couch. There was a brown bean-bag chair, and an angular black metal chair with a white canvas sling to sit in. A hall went off to my left, and through an open archway beyond the suede couch I could see the kitchen.

"Please have a seat," she said. "I'll get you some wine."

She was gone for a minute and when she came back she was carrying a big jug of white wine and a glass. There was a marble-top coffee table in front of the couch, the marble marked with a large number of circular stains where glasses had been set down without coasters. She set my glass and hers on the coffee table and poured me some wine, and some for herself, holding the jug in both hands. There was no air-conditioning and the bottle was already beginning to sweat in the hot room. I had a sip of wine. It wasn't very good, but it would probably prevent plaque. Car-lotta raised her glass toward me and drank some.

"Good times," she said.

"So," I said, "tell me about Jerome."

"Why?"

I didn't want to appear unsociable; I drank a little more of the jug wine. My shirt was already beginning to stick to my back.

"He and I are supposed to do a little, ah, business."

I smiled what I hoped was a cryptic smile. Susan had told me that sometimes my cryptic smile shaded off into a leer, which had shaken my confidence in it. But this time it seemed to work.

"Business?" she said.

"Yes. Him and Tino. They told me to come here."

"You know Tino?"

"Sure."

She had finished her wine already and was pouring another large, clumsy dose from the jug. When she leaned forward I could see that she wore no bra, which was much more information than I really wanted.

"Tino and Jerome and I were supposed to do a piece of business," I said, "for Jerome's boss, what'sisname?"

Carlotta was looking at me speculatively over her wine glass. Sweat added sheen to her forehead and glimmered faintly on her upper lip.

"Mister Tannenbaum," she said absently.

"Yeah, Tannenbaum, and they told me to meet them here."

"Anyone ever tell you that you're a cutie?" Carlotta said.

"Jerome and Tino just said that last night."

She smiled automatically and drank some wine.

"Well you are, and don't you just know it."

"When do you expect Jerome back?" I said.

"He went to the beach for a few days," she said. "You ever fool around?"

"No. I always mean it," I said.

"Maybe you oughta," she said.

I would have been more flattered if I had the sense that she didn't proposition everyone she met. And if she wasn't drunk. And, the ugly sexist truth of the matter, if her thighs weren't flabby.

"You know where Mr. Tannenbaum lives?" I said.

"Lives? How the hell would I know where he lives? You think he invites me and Jerome over for cocktails? I never even met him."

"But he's in L.A. someplace," I said.

She drank some wine and nodded.

"Me and Jerome never get invited anyplace. We eat cheap, we drink cheap, we live in this dump and Jerome don't even pay the rent."

She began to tear up.

"Wasn't for my alimony check we couldn't even live like we do," she said.

Her wine glass was empty. She did another two-handed pour from the jug and spilled some of it on the coffee table and began to cry.

"You wanna fuck me or not," she said through the tears.

"Anyone would," I said. "But I can't."

"Why not?"

I made a cryptic gesture and smiled a cryptic smile and stood up. When I did I could see myself in the oval mirror that hung over the gas log fire place on the far wall. My cryptic smile was not very convincing. It looked a little panicky. My face was sweaty. If I did not know and admire the owner, it was not a face I'd like very much.

"Whyn't you sit, drink some wine, have a little fun."

"I wish I could," I said.

"But you're uptight," she said.

"That's it," I said. "Thanks for the wine."

She was looking into her near-empty wine glass now, with her feet flat on the floor and her shoulders hunched as if she were cold, which was not possible in the stifling room.

"Get lost," she said.

Which I did.

chapter
30

VINCENT DEL RIO had an estate in Bel Air where he was master of all he surveyed, and a good deal more than that. The place was about the size of Worcester, Massachusetts, and a lot better looking in its flowery green Southern-California way.

Even though I had called first, I had to do a lot of explaining to a sequence of scary-looking men of Mexican lineage as I worked my way past the gate, and past the front door, and into the courtyard of his vast white-stucco-and-red-tile home, into the presence of Vincent del Rio.

"Señor Spenser," he said.

Del Rio was wearing a white suit today with a crimson silk shirt open at the neck.

I said, "Jefe."

Del Rio smiled and sipped from a glass of iced tea. Bobby Horse was leaning against the courtyard wall with his thick arms folded. He nodded at me. I nodded back. Chollo was there, seated with del Rio under an olive tree, at a round, red wood table with a brick-colored tile top. They were playing chess. Chollo was as he had been, still medium height and slender, with his long hair in a ponytail. Even seated, he managed to look languid, which he wasn't. On the table were a pitcher of iced tea and a dish of sliced lemons, several glasses, and the chessboard.

"Sit down," del Rio said.

I sat between him and Chollo.

Chollo said, "Amigo."

I said, "Chollo."

"You want some iced tea?" del Rio said.

"Gracias."

"Cut the crap," del Rio said. "What do you want?"

He had no trace of an accent.

"Two sugars, some lemon."

Chollo pushed the pitcher over toward me.

"Help yourself," del Rio said.

I fixed myself up some iced tea and took a sip.

"Mango," I said. "Very good."

Nobody said anything. Del Rio folded his hands across his stomach and leaned back in his chair. He looked sort of stagy, like an Anglo playing a Mexican, with a Pancho Villa moustache and his dark hair slicked back.

"Family okay?" I said.

"Yes, my daughter is married now and lives in La Jolla."

"You approve?" I said.

"If I did not, it would not have happened."

"Husband in your business?" I said.

"No. He is a marine biologist."

"Does he know your line of work?" I said.

"He did not marry me," del Rio said. "You have business with me?"

A small fountain made a soft falling-water sound in one corner.

"I need two favors."

"Perhaps you're confused," del Rio said. "This is not Travelers Aid."

"One, I'm interested in a guy named Tannenbaum," I said.

Del Rio looked up from his chessboard.

"Really?" he said. "Why?"

"A guy who works for him threatened to beat me up the other night on Olympic Boulevard."

"And?"

"And he didn't," I said. "But I'd sort of like to know why."

"I can see why you would," del Rio said. "But why do I care what you'd like?"

"Because I'm a fine person?"

"Do you know the name of the man who threatened to beat you up?"

"Jerome Jefferson," I said. "Guy with him called Tino."

Del Rio shook his head. He looked at Chollo. Chollo shrugged.

"We don't know them," del Rio said.

"Small-time guys," I said. "Don't waste the name players on a stiff from Boston."

Del Rio nodded.

"It is good that you understand your position here," he said.

"How about Tannenbaum?" I said. "Is he a name player?"

"Yes."

"Tell me about him."

"First," del Rio said, "you tell me what you might be doing that would come to Morris Tannenbaum's attention?"

"I'm working on a murder case," I said.

"Here?"

"Some people involved used to live here," I said. "But the murder was out in the desert, place called Potshot."

Del Rio moved one of the chess pieces.

"Is there a connection?"

"I don't know."

"Of course you don't," del Rio said.

Chollo moved a chess piece. Del Rio studied the move. I don't play chess. I had no idea what they were doing.

"Morris is an important figure in this part of the country."

"As important as you?" I said.

Del Rio consulted the chess book and studied the board and moved another piece.

"Not to me," he said.

"Me either," I said. "What's Tannenbaum do for a living?"

Del Rio smiled.

"He's a venture capitalist," del Rio said. "Like me."

"What's he invest in?"

"Drugs, whores, numbers . . . usual thing."

"Competition?" I said.

"Not really," del Rio said. "He operates east of Chino."

"The inland empire?"

Del Rio nodded, studying the chessboard.

"Fresno," he said. "Bakersfield, San Berdoo, Riverside."

"Where would I find him?"

Del Rio moved a chess piece, kept his hand on it for a moment, and moved it back. He continued to stare at the board. Chollo was motionless.

"Palm Springs," del Rio said.

"Maybe I should go out and talk with him."

Del Rio smiled and moved a chess piece, sat back, and looked at the move with satisfaction.

"It would save you the drive if you were to shoot yourself here."

"Morris is not friendly."

"No."

"Is he persistent?"

"Very."

"So he'll admonish me again," I said.

Del Rio looked at Chollo.

"Admonish," he said.

"Even for a gringo he talks funny," Chollo said.

"Yes," del Rio said. "He will admonish you again."

"So maybe I'll need backup," I said.

Del Rio looked again at Chollo. Chollo was studying the board. Without looking away he said, "Backup."

"That would be the second favor," del Rio said.

"Sí."

"You wish to borrow Chollo?"

"Like last time," I said. "And Bobby Horse, too. If you would."

Del Rio leaned back in his chair and stared at me.

"They are not mine to lend," he said.

"Then, I'd like your permission to make them a proposal."

Again the silence and the stare. Chollo looked amused. Against the wall Bobby Horse showed nothing. His strong-featured Indian face was entirely blank.

Finally del Rio said, "That is respectful."

"I'm a respectful guy," I said.

"In this instance," del Rio said.

A small bird with a black back made small syncopated noise in the olive tree.

Del Rio looked at Chollo and then at Bobby Horse.

"Do you wish to listen to his proposal?" he said.

"Sí," Chollo said.

Bobby Horse shrugged and nodded.

"I need some help with this guy Tannenbaum," I said. "And I need a few hard cases to go out to the desert with me and clean up a town."

"Clean up the criminal element?" Chollo said.

"Yeah."

"We *are* the criminal element," Chollo said.

"Yeah, but you're not *their* criminal element."

"What do you want with Tannenbaum?" Chollo said.

"I don't know. But it must have something to do with the thing in the desert."

"So you clean up one, you clean up the other?"

"Sí."

"I didn't realize you spoke our language," Chollo said.

"Sí."

"If you were to succeed in this," del Rio said. "It might provide me an opportunity to expand eastward."

"If Tannenbaum went down," I said.

"Sí."

I looked at Chollo.

"He's fluent too," I said.

"Tannenbaum don't bother me none," Chollo said. "What

about the desert business? You figure your criminal element can beat their criminal element?"

"That's my plan," I said.

"How big is their criminal element?"

"Thirty, forty guys."

"And ours?"

"With you and Bobby Horse," I said. "There would be seven."

"Including you?"

"Including me," I said. "Which really makes it seventeen. As you know, my strength is as the strength of ten."

"Ten what?" Chollo said.

"You paying?" Bobby Horse said.

"Big time," I said.

"How much?"

I told him. He looked at Chollo.

"I saved his ass once before," Chollo said. "He's sort of fun for an Anglo."

Bobby Horse looked at del Rio.

"Mr. del Rio?"

"I don't have a problem with it," del Rio said. "Chollo?"

"No problem."

"Okay," Bobby Horse said.

"Can you make the phone call?" I said to del Rio. "To Tannenbaum. I want to visit him without being fired upon as I come up the driveway."

"I'll have it made," he said.

"Gracias."

Del Rio grinned.

"Sí," he said.

chapter
31

IN A DARK brown Range Rover, laden with brush gear and sonorous with stereo, with Bobby Horse driving and Chollo beside him, and me in the back seat, we cruised down Palm Canyon Drive, through Palm Springs on Racquet Club Road and into Morris Tannenbaum's circular crushed stone driveway. Beyond the house a golf course rolled toward the mountain. The house itself was modest for Palm Springs, with the usual stuccoed walls and red-tiled roof. It looked like a dozen other homes with access to the golf course, except for the tastefully understated security cameras, and the black Lincoln Towncar that sat outside with its motor running. Chollo took a Derringer from the glove compartment and put it over the sun visor. We parked beside the Lincoln. After a moment the door opened on the passenger side and a tall leathery guy in a cowboy hat and Oakley shades got out and walked over to us. Chollo lowered his window. The cowboy looked in at me in the back.

"'That him?" he said.

"Sí," Chollo said.

The cowboy looked at me some more, then straightened and jerked his head toward the house.

"Okay," he said.

Bobby Horse shut off the motor and we got out into the heat, walked to the front door, and rang the bell. A Filipino house boy answered and bowed us into the air-conditioned hallway.

"Please to wait here," he said and went down the hall and disappeared. In a few moments a man came out of the door where the Filipino had gone and walked to us. He was a well-built guy, like a racquetball player, or a tennis pro. He had a crew cut. He was wearing a blue seersucker suit, and a blue oxford shirt with a button-down collar, a blue-and-red-striped tie, and horn-rimmed glasses. As he came down the hallway he was looking at Chollo. I glanced over. Chollo was looking at him. When he reached us he stopped. Still looking at Chollo, he said, "You wish to see Morris?"

"Yes," I said.

"Five minutes," he said.

"Plenty," I said.

Chollo and the suit continued to look at each other.

Then the suit said, "Follow me," and turned and went back down the hall. We followed him into a smallish room that looked out through glass doors at a modest pool, and beyond, to the green of the golf course. A big-screen television set on a high shelf was blasting out a rollicking symphony of canned laughter. The room was full of exercise equipment, Nautilus, Kaiser,

Cybex; a complete set of chrome-plated free weights. A flabby unshaven guy in a yellow sweatsuit was doing assisted dips on a Gravitron. There was a stair-climber and an exercycle, and a treadmill all arranged so that they faced the television. The bicycle had a reading stand attached and around it, on the floor, were scattered parts of the *Los Angeles Times* and *The Wall Street Journal*. Several half-consumed bottles of Gatorade stood around. One had tipped over and was puddling the floor. The man on the Gravitron had a thick crop of dark black hair. His unshaven stubble was gray. The contrast was a little suspicious. I noticed that the counterweight on the Gravitron was set as high as it would go, which meant that he was dipping very little weight.

"Ronny," the man said, still on the Gravitron, "the room's a fucking mess."

Without a word, the suit who let us in went to a desk beside the door and pressed a button. The flabby guy climbed down off the Gravitron and wiped his face with a towel and took a big pull of Gatorade.

"I'm Morris Tannenbaum," the flabby guy said. "Whaddya want?"

The Filipino came silently into the room and folded up the newspapers, picked up the Gatorade bottles, cleaned up the spill and went silently out. Ronny stayed by the door looking at Chollo, who was looking at him. Bobby Horse stood just behind me, motionless. I glanced at him. His face had no expression.

"My name's Spenser," I said. "I wonder why you sent Jerome Jefferson and his friend Tino to scare me out of my wits."

"Don't know Tino," Tannenbaum said. "Jerome must have recruited him. I sent Jerome because I thought he could take care of things. I was wrong."

"What things did you want taken care of?"

"I want you to forget about Steve Buckman. I want you to stay away from Lou Buckman, and I want you to forget about the Dell."

"Un-huh."

"And if you don't do what I want I'll have you killed."

"How come?" I said.

"Because I say so, that's how come. You think because you get del Rio to call me, and you bring a couple of his greasers to back you up, that somehow makes you different from every other two-bit cheapie I've put in the fucking ground?"

"I'm the greaser," Chollo said, still looking at Ronnie. He tilted his head toward Bobby Horse. "He's an Indian."

Tannenbaum made a little dismissive gesture with his hand, and kept his eyes on me.

"You heard me," he said.

"I did, and I'm trying to get my breath back," I said.

"Okay," Tannenbaum said. "You been told. Straight up. From me to you. Beat it."

"What's your interest in Lou Buckman?" I said. "Or the Dell?"

"This is my home," Tannenbaum said. "I do not wish to kill you here. But I'll kill you somewhere, and soon."

Tannenbaum got up and walked out. Ronnie went out after him and closed the door. In another minute the Filipino came in.

"May I show you out?" he said.

I said he might. We got back in the car, drove back out to Route 10, and headed for L.A., past the Indian bingo parlors and the places that sold Famous Date Shakes.

"Ronny looks sort of like an accountant," I said to Chollo.

"He's not," Chollo said.

"No," I said. "He's not. You think Tannenbaum will try to kill me?"

"In your language," Chollo said, "you bet your ass."

"Well it's been tried before," I said.

"You want me to kill him?" Chollo said.

"No. But I might take a rain check."

"What's the Dell?" Bobby Horse said.

"You don't know," I said.

"I did would I be asking?"

"But Tannenbaum did," I said.

"So his interest is not just what'shername," Chollo said.

"Lou Buckman. No. It's Potshot."

"So, what's the Dell," Bobby Horse said.

I told him.

"Tannenbaum connected with this Preacher hombre, maybe?" Chollo said.

"Hombre?" I said.

"Just like to stay authentic to my heritage," Chollo said.

"Chollo, you grew up in East L.A.," I said.

"And I'm true to my heritage," Chollo said. "I am a thug."

"And a good one," I said.

"A thing worth doing," Chollo said, "is worth doing well."

"You got a plan?" Bobby Horse said.

"I can't seem to connect any of the dots," I said, "so, I think I'll blunder around out here some more. Something's got to be connected to someone."

"There's a connection," Chollo said. "You just don't know what it is."

"Story of my sleuthing career," I said.

chapter
32

ONE OF THE things I always liked, especially when I traveled with Susan, was to have breakfast with her. The only drawback was that, no matter when you woke up, you waited an hour or so to eat while she worked out, showered, did her hair, put on her face and dressed like a Parisian model. I had never actually met a Parisian model, but I was sure that if I did, she'd be dressed like Susan. The thing was that without her clothes on, with no makeup, and her hair down, she was gorgeous. Occasionally I remarked about carrying coals to Newcastle. And always, when I did, she gave me a look of such penetrating pity that I never pursued it.

The way we normally worked it was that she said she'd meet me in the dining room at, say, 9 A.M. and I should go down and get a table for us. So I would and have some juice and coffee and study the menu and she would show up about 9:30 without any apparent awareness that she was a half-hour late. On the other hand she wasn't reliable. If I went down at 9:30 she would have showed up before me, and, in the future, would expect me to be a half-hour late. So next time, she'd show up at 10.

It is one of the secrets of happiness that you know which battles you can win and which you can't. I had given up the punctuality battle years ago. And the pleasure of her company when she did show up was always worth the wait.

I had drunk some orange juice and read *USA Today*, and was on my second cup of coffee at a table for two, near a window, when she came gleaming into the dining room. Several people looked at her more or less covertly. Maybe she was a movie star.

"I'm sorry I'm late," she said.

"Really?" I said. "I didn't notice."

"Do you know what you're going to have?" she said.

"Here's a how-well-do-you-know-me test," I said. "Read the menu, see if you can guess."

Susan put on the reading glasses she had just bought on Rodeo Drive, round ones with bright green frames, and studied the menu. She smiled.

"Ah ha!" she said.

"And your answer is?"

"Heuevos rancheros," she said.

"You win," I said.

"Good. What have I won?"

I smiled at her without speaking.

"Oh," Susan said, "that."

When the waiter arrived, Susan ordered decaffeinated coffee, and a fresh fruit platter with yogurt. I kept my date with the heuevos rancheros.

"Other than a threat to my life the other night outside that restaurant," Susan said, "I've been having a very nice time. How about you?"

"The time we've spent together has been nice," I said.

"Isn't it always," Susan said.

"But other than that I feel like the more I learn the less I know."

"Do you know who it was that threatened us?"

"Guy named Jerome Jefferson," I said, "sent by a man named Morris Tannenbaum."

"How about the other man? Tino?"

"No record. Haven't located him. The guess is he's a day player, hired by Jefferson for the occasion."

The food arrived. Susan ate a raspberry.

"Why would this Tannenbaum person want to threaten us?"

"He wants me to stay away from Lou Buckman, Potshot, the Dell, and the west side of the continent."

"He mentioned the Dell?"

"Yep."

"Then he's . . . he's involved," she said.

"You get sick of shrinkage, you could get a license and join me. Spenser and Silverman, investigations."

She picked up a wedge of cantaloupe with her fingers and took a small bite off of the end of it. I could never figure out why I was eating with my hands when I did that. When she did it she was elegant.

"Alphabetically it's Silverman and Spenser," she said.

"But I'd be senior partner."

"And I'd be main squeeze," she said.

"Silverman and Spenser," I said. "Investigations."

"So how is Tannenbaum involved?"

"I don't know."

"Have you learned anything more about Lou Buckman, the little blonde cutie?"

"You sound jealous," I said.

"So?"

"You haven't even met her."

"So?"

"Apparently all was not as it seemed with the Buckmans. They don't seem to be too well liked by former colleagues and neighbors. It is alleged that they both slept around. One interesting factoid: Both Mark Ratliff and Dean Walker lived in the Buckmans' old neighborhood in Santa Monica. Ratliff seems to have had an affair with her. And the former Mrs. Ratliff had a get-even affair with Steve Buckman."

"Walker is the police chief in Potshot," Susan said. "Who's Ratliff?"

"I told you about him," I said. "The producer. Moved to Potshot to get away from the Hollywood rat race."

Susan smiled.

"Where, I assume, he was running a dead last."

"I've heard," I said, "that people with a three-picture deal don't usually seem to suffer the same moral revulsion."

Susan dipped a small wedge of pineapple into her small cup of yogurt and took a small bite.

"So what are you going to do now?"

"When in doubt," I said, "go home."

"Oh good," Susan said.

"Getting bored?"

"Getting homesick," Susan said.

"Pearl?" I said.

"Yes. I miss her."

"Yeah. You talk with Farrell at all?"

"Of course. He says she's sleeping with him every night. Says it's his first female."

"Man is she easy," I said.

"She's just a friendly girl," Susan said.

chapter
33

I⟨T WAS SEPTEMBER⟩ in Boston, which normally means early fall. When I went to work the morning after I got home, the day was bright blue and 70 degrees. The first hint of color was beginning to show in the leaves of some trees. Once again pennant fever was not gripping the Hub. And there wasn't a starlet in sight.

My first assignment was to catch up. Catching up meant mostly throwing away junk mail without reading it. But there was my answering machine to listen to. Since I'd been gone there were eight new messages. One was from Frank Belson inviting me and Susan to have dinner with him and Lisa. One was from a young Chinese girl named Mei Ling who wanted to use me as a job reference. One was from Samuelson in L.A. with instructions to call him.

"Couple of sheriff's deputies found your pal, Jerome Jefferson,"

Samuelson said when I got him, "beside the PCH up near Topanga Canyon."

"Dead?" I said.

"Nine millimeter, once, behind his left ear."

"Think it happened there or was he dumped?"

"Coroner says he was dumped."

"Suspects?"

"None."

"Leads?"

"None."

"Clues?"

"Come on!"

"Chances of solving this?"

Samuelson laughed.

"Around zilch," he said.

"Tannenbaum?" I said.

"Probably," Samuelson said. "Wasn't satisfied with Jerome's job performance."

"There's a girlfriend on Franklin Avenue," I said. "She might know something."

"Name and address?"

I told him.

"Get there early," I said. "She should be drunk by noon."

"Wish I were."

"Cop's life is a hard one," I said. "Could you get me the record of a former cop named Dean Walker? Used to live in Santa Monica. I don't know if he was LAPD or Santa Monica."

"Glad to," Samuelson said. "If I didn't have legwork for you, I wouldn't have anything to do."

"Thank you."

"You're welcome," Samuelson said.

"Call me when you know something. If I'm not here, leave it on my machine. I may be traveling.

"Pay attention while you are," Samuelson said. "Morris Tannenbaum is a genuine bad guy. The real thing."

"All the way to Boston?" I said.

"Wherever," Samuelson said. "If he thinks it's a good thing to do."

"Lot of people think it's a good thing to do," I said. "I'm still here."

"Don't let it go to your head," Samuelson said and hung up.

I listened to the rest of my messages. All of them were from Potshot. Two from Lou Buckman. Two from Roscoe Land, the Potshot mayor. And one from Luther Barnes. All of them were wondering how things were going and when I might come back there with my colleagues and clean up the Dell. I didn't return the calls.

chapter
34

PEARL WAS AGING. Her muzzle was gray, her hearing was less acute, her eyesight wasn't as good as it used to be and her left front shoulder was arthritic, causing her to limp when she walked. But she was a hunting dog, and the genes persist. She could still track an open packet of peanut butter Nabs across any terrain.

"Not too much longer," Susan said, watching Pearl ease up onto the couch. "Pretty soon we'll have to boost her."

We were drinking Iron Horse champagne in Susan's living room. Tomorrow I was heading to Potshot and the farewell supper that Susan had made waited on the counter in her kitchen, blocked off by chairs. Pearl hadn't lost that much.

"We won't mind," I said.

"No," Susan said.

"What's for supper?"

She smiled.

"Do you ask out of eagerness or fear?"

"Just looking for information," I said.

"Lobster salad and corn."

"Native corn?"

"Yes, from Verrill farm."

"Prepared by you?" I said.

"I bought the lobster salad," Susan said. "I was hoping you'd boil the corn."

Pearl didn't like the position she had assumed on the couch. She stood and turned around a couple of times and lay back down, as far as I could tell, in the same position, and sighed with relief.

"I already have to boost her onto the bed."

"Isn't she kind of heavy?" I said.

"Yes," Susan said.

Susan usually hung around the house in sweats that cost more than my suit, and looked better. But she had her own sense of occasion and tonight, because I was going away for awhile, she wore a little black dress, and pearls. Her arms and shoulders and neck were strong. Her makeup was perfect. Her face was dominated by her eyes. Her face hinted strongly at intelligence and heat. *Excellent combination*.

"I heard somebody define heaven once," she said, looking at Pearl, "as a place where, when you get there, all the dogs you ever loved run to greet you."

"As good as any," I said.

She sipped her champagne. Pearl shifted a little on the couch and lapped her nose a couple of times.

"Do you think there's anything after death?" Susan said.

"Yikes," I said.

"No. Talk about it. Surely doing what you do, you've thought about it."

"As little as possible," I said.

"But you've thought about it."

"Sure."

"And?"

I took in a little champagne.

"There are some scientists," I said, "who've discovered an element of light that is faster than light."

"Einstein said that's not possible," Susan said.

"It arrives at the receiver before it leaves the transmitter," I said.

"What about cause and effect?"

I shrugged.

"Afterlife is no less implausible than anything else," I said. "All explanations of existence are equally incredible."

"So you might as well believe something that makes you feel good as not," Susan said.

"No harm to it," I said.

We were quiet, drinking champagne, looking at Pearl, who had fallen asleep.

"Well," Susan said, "we'll find out someday."

"Or we won't," I said, "in which case we won't know it."

Susan's glass was empty. She held it out to me. I took the Champagne from the ice bucket and poured her another dollop.

"I don't know whether you've cheered me up or depressed me," Susan said.

"If your feelings are inspired by Pearl's forthcoming demise, I can offer a less-complex solution."

"I know."

"Mourn for an appropriate time. . . ." I said.

"And buy another brown German shorthair," Susan said, "and name her Pearl."

"Reincarnation," I said.

"Maybe I'm not just thinking about Pearl," Susan said.

"Is it Margaret that you mourn for?" I said.

"No," Susan said.

"Does it have anything to do with me leaving for Potshot tomorrow?"

"Yes."

"Would drinking and eating and making love ease your concerns?" I said.

Susan smiled at me.

"Oddly enough," she said, "it would."

It made me feel pretty good too.

chapter
35

Hawk had acquired a black Ford Explorer, properly registered with a new inspection sticker. I didn't ask him about it. He and I and Vinnie, with gear, were on the road the next day by 8:00 in the morning. Hawk was driving. Vinnie was in the back seat. The sun was shining directly into our faces. I was drinking coffee and eating two donuts. Donuts make excellent travel food.

"We coulda flown," Vinnie said. "Take us four or five hours."

"With a bunch of infernal devices?" Hawk said.

"You mean guns?" Vinnie said.

"Sho 'nuff," Hawk said.

"Hell," Vinnie said. "You coulda driven the guns out, and I coulda flown out next week, first class, and met you there."

"We may all wish you did," I said. "An hour out of Boston and you're already bitching."

Vinnie almost smiled.

"We there yet?" he said.

I had a CD in the player. Carol Sloane and Clark Terry.

"She can sing for a white broad," Hawk said.

"The best," I said.

"Keeps right up with the black guy," Hawk said.

"Astonishing isn't it?" I said.

We turned off the Mass Pike at Sturbridge and went west on Route 84. We weren't in a hurry. We drove through Connecticut, which was low and green and suburban. We went across New York state and crossed the Hudson River near Fishkill. We crossed the Delaware near Port Jervis and after awhile picked up Route 81 at Scranton. The country had grown hillier. We played CDs: Carol Sloan, and Sarah, and Bob Stewart, and Sinatra, Mel Torme, and Ella, and some Clifford Brown. Hawk insisted on a couple of Afro-Cuban CDs that gave me a stomachache, but I tried to stay open-minded. We talked about sex and baseball, and food and drink, and the days when Hawk and I were fighters. When we exhausted that topic we talked about sex, and basketball, and the days when we were soldiers. We stopped along the way for more coffee, and more donuts, and peanut butter Nabs, and prewrapped ham sandwiches, and pre-condimented cheeseburgers, and chicken deep-fried in cholesterol.

"We got to find better chop," Hawk said. "We keep eating this crap we'll be dead before we get there."

"Maybe the next place will have a salad bar," I said.

"With some of that orange French dressing," Hawk said.

"Which is also excellent for slicking your hair back."

"My hair?" Hawk said.

"If you had some."

"Used to have an Afro," Hawk said.

"I remember," I said. "You looked like a short Artis Gilmore."

"Handsome," Hawk said, "and distinguished, but too easy to get hold of in a scuffle. My present do is more practical."

In the back Vinnie looked out the window and said very little. Vinnie wasn't much for small talk.

We stopped the first night at Hagerstown, Maryland, near the Antietam battlefield, and slept in a Holiday Inn. We drove south. We listened to Tony Bennett and Carmen McRea, Anita O'Day, Stan Kenton, Bobby Hackett and Johnny Hartman.

Going through West Virginia, near Martinsburg, Vinnie said, "You guys ever listen to anything recorded this century?"

Hawk said, "No."

"Don't you have nothing like Pink Floyd, or Procol Harum?"

"How 'bout The Ink Spots?" Hawk said.

Vinnie shook his head and settled back to look out the window.

We drove down the horsy green Shenandoah Valley with the Alleghenies to the west and Blue Ridge to the east. We hit Knoxville that evening. We crossed the Mississippi at Memphis a day later. Fort Smith, Little Rock, Oklahoma City. I felt like Bobby Troup. Shoney's, Shakey's, McDonald's, Burger King, KFC. I felt my arteries clogging. Gulf, Mobile, Esso, Pilot. Truck stops with buffet tables where you could overeat vastly for maybe six bucks. Hawk and I had a running bet as to who could count the most desirable women. By the time we crossed the Texas panhandle I had already spotted two. Hawk said it wasn't fair, that my standards were too low.

"You have to adjust," I said, "to your environment."

We went through Amarillo. Big John's Steak House. Tucumcari. Uphill to Albuquerque. We slept in Holiday Inns, and Quality Courts, and Hampton Courts, and Motel Sixes. We drank coffee and Coke and bottled water. We pulled into rest stops and mingled with fat people who wore pink shorts and plastic baseball caps. I was leading the desirable woman contest two to one. Sometimes the people wore plaid shorts and plastic baseball caps. They were of both genders, I think. Motor homes got in our way. They moved like odd beetles, slowly, hugging the edge of the highway, driven uneasily by aging people, many of whom were almost certainly wearing pink shorts. Big rigs with fifteen gears slowed us down on the upgrades, and tore past us on the downgrades, trying to make time, which as we know, is money. Small sub sandwiches, biscuits and gravy. Biscuits and sausage. Biscuits and sausage with gravy. Chicken fried steak with cream gravy.

"Used to sleep with a woman was a professor at Harvard," Hawk said. "Red-headed woman. Taught *literature*."

I was driving. Hawk was in the passenger seat. Vinnie was in the back seat gazing out the window.

"She felt I was," and his voice deepened and his accent disappeared, *"the perfect embodiment of untrammeled sensuality. Unrestrained by the stale ethics or conventions of the state."*

"I thought that was you," I said.

"What the fuck she talking about?" Vinnie said.

"Meant she liked a lot of unusual ways to do it," Hawk said.

"Nothing wrong with that," Vinnie said.

"Nuthin'," Hawk said.

The next morning we came down out of the mountains west of Albuquerque, and by evening were in the desert.

chapter
36

THE HOUSE WAS on the east edge of town, with a good view out the back windows of the Sawtooths to the east. It was a big sprawling place with a wide front porch. Bernard J. Fortunato was on the front porch when we pulled up. He was wearing a red-checked shirt and blue jeans and a cowboy hat and boots. A blue bandanna was knotted around his throat.

"Who the fuck is that," Vinnie said, "Roy Rogers?"

"It's that tough little dude from Vegas," Hawk said.

"Bernard J. Fortunato," I said. "We're all gathering. It'll be like *The Big Chill*."

"Just like," Hawk said.

"About time you got here," Bernard said. "I been cooling my heels in this burg for a couple days now."

"Been shopping some," Hawk said.

"Yeah. Hawk, how ya doing. Good to see ya again."

I introduced Vinnie, who already had the rear lid of the Explorer open and was starting to unload. And we carried everything into the house. It was sort of shabby inside, but big. Six bedrooms and two baths upstairs, and a big study downstairs that would convert to a bedroom. There was also a living room, a dining room, a large kitchen, another full bath, and central air.

"Furnished," Bernard said. "Six bills a month, large."

"Six grand a month?" I said. "We better clean this up quick."

"Hey that's with the furniture, all the pots and pans, all we got to do is pay the fucking utilities."

"Anybody else show up yet?" I said.

"The hard case from Atlanta pulled in yesterday," Bernard said. "Where do you find these guys?"

"I pick them up at Tony Robbins Seminars," I said. "Where's Sapp?"

"Out running," Bernard said.

"It's a hundred and ten thousand fucking degrees," Vinnie said. Bernard shrugged.

"What have we got for bedrooms?" I said.

"Sapp's upstairs, front," Bernard said. "I took the couch in the den. I'm compact, and I don't sleep much anyway."

"Compact," Hawk said.

We took our luggage, left the other gear on the floor in the living room, and located ourselves in bedrooms. I took a front bedroom where you could overlook the town. There was a double bed with maple headboard and footboard and fluted posts with wooden flames at the top at each corner, a maple dresser and a disreputable looking gray-and-black steamer trunk at the foot of the bed. The windows had shades, but no curtains. Normally when I travel, I don't unpack, but I was going to be here a bit, so I put my stuff in the maple bureau, and went back down-stairs. Bernard, Tedy Sapp, Hawk and Vinnie were sitting on the wide porch in the cooling evening, having a drink.

"You want something?" Bernard said.

He had set up a little drink table on the porch, with ice in a bucket. I made myself a Scotch and soda and sat down.

"I guess you've all met."

"We have," Sapp said. "Two more coming?"

"Yeah, driving over from L.A."

"Desert cools off good in the dark doesn't it," Sapp said. "Georgia it's hot all night."

"Hope the a/c keep pumping," Hawk said.

"It don't I can fix it," Vinnie said.

"You know how to fix air-conditioners?" Hawk said.

"Anything," Vinnie said. "Cars, machine guns, phones, TVs. I can fix shit."

We all looked at Vinnie as if he had just come out of the closet. He shrugged. We drank our drinks and sat quietly. The desert air was clear and the stars were bigger than I was used to. A night bird kept chirping something that sounded like "tuck-a-hoo."

I felt like singing "Home on the Range."

"You hungry?" Sapp asked.

"The drive out was a movable feast," I said. "Why would we be hungry?"

"I made a meatloaf," Sapp said, "and there's some beans."

"Well aren't you the homebody," Hawk said.

"Yeah. Bernie hated my pink apron," Sapp said. "Straight guys are so fucking straight."

"Bernard," Fortunato said.

"There's biscuits, too," Sapp said.

chapter
37

I WAS IN THE Chiricahuas County Sheriff's Department talking with their chief homicide investigator. The room was cinderblock. The windows were tinted. The air-conditioning was high. The metal desk and chairs and file cabinet and small conference table were forest green, perfectly complementing the light green walls. All of it was brightly lit by a bank of overhead fluorescents, which perfectly complemented the sunlight coming in through the windows. The chief investigator's name was Cawley Dark. He was a thin, leathery-looking guy wearing starched blue jeans and snakeskin cowboy boots, a white oxford shirt with the sleeves rolled up and a Glock 9, high on his waist just in front of his right hip. On the forest green metal bookcase behind his desk was a big photograph of three teenaged girls clustering around a blond horse with a white mane.

"Buckman was shot three times," he said. "With a 9-millimeter weapon. We did an autopsy, couldn't match the slugs to anything. Wife says he was threatened by some people from the Dell. We say, 'Who?' She says, 'I don't know.' We say, 'Would you recognize them?' She says, 'Certainly.' "

"Pick up anyone from the Dell?" I said.

Dark smiled.

"Everybody we picked up was from the Dell," he said. "It's what we use for a ghetto, out here."

"And?"

"And she says none of them are the guys. She thinks."

"Anybody else look at them?"

"Nope."

"He got shot in the middle of the day on the main street in Potshot and no one saw anything."

"Amazing isn't it," Dark said.

"You have any reason to believe it wasn't the way it's been described?" I said.

"Nothing I know says it didn't happen that way," Dark said.

"But?"

"But nothing I know says it's right." Dark said. "You want coffee?"

"No thanks."

He got up and went to a coffee maker on top of the file cabinet and poured himself some coffee from a stained pot, and came back and sat down. He took a sip and shuddered.

"Goddamn that's awful," he said.

"Glad I declined," I said.

"After you called," Dark said, "I checked on you in Boston. Got booted around a little. Ended up talking to a state guy named Healy."

"One of my biggest fans," I said.

Dark made a wobbling metz metz gesture with his right hand.

"What do you think about Potshot?" he said.

"A mess," I said. "What do you think of the police chief down there?"

"Walker? Odd duck. I don't know how good he is but he's better than anyone else. The last two quit and left the area."

"Always been a small force?"

"No," Dark said. "For awhile they had an actual police force. Then one of them got killed. And most of the rest sort of dropped out and went away, one at a time."

"Who killed him?"

"Probably the Dell, but we have no evidence."

"Why don't you roust them out of there anyway?" I said.

Dark grinned.

"I'm just a homicide cop," he said. "That's SWAT team stuff."

"And why doesn't the SWAT team do it?"

"Got no legal basis for it for one thing," he said. "Far as we can prove, nobody in the Dell has committed an indictable offense. And just, to complicate things, The Preacher claims that the Dell is a religious organization and any effort to control them is an abridgement of their religious freedom."

"And no one wants to get in to another Waco situation," I said.

"You bet," Dark said.

"So you think Walker is in the bag?" I said.

"With the Dell? He's survived in a job that no one seems able to keep."

"You feel the others were run off by the Dell?"

"That's what I figure," Dark said.

"And you can't prove it?"

"Nope. Even talked to one of the previous police chiefs, fella named Mizell. He wasn't talking about anything. But he seemed to be living comfortable."

"You think they bribed him?"

"I had to guess," Dark said, "I think they did both. They told him if he stuck around they'd kill him, so he left. But to keep him quiet, they give him a separation bonus."

"But Walker has stayed," I said.

"Yep. He's either tougher than a rabid skunk," Dark said. "Or . . ."

"Or they like him just the way he is," I said.

"Maybe they figured they couldn't keep running these guys off without one of them deciding to testify. They're paying them off anyway, so they got a guy they didn't need to run off, and paid him to stay and keep his mouth shut." Dark said.

"Or maybe he's just stubborn," I said.

"I'd be more likely to believe that if he was dead."

"Cynical," I said.

"Probably. You alone?"

"No, I have a few friends with me," I said.

"According to Healy you can't help yourself. You'll annoy The Preacher enough so sooner or later he'll take a run at you."

"Guys just like to have fun," I said.

"Well if they kill you, try and get them to leave clues around," Dark said. "I'd love to bust everybody down there."

chapter 38

IT WAS TIME to confer with our employers, and, since we were hoping to keep our profile low, we invited them to our place.

It was a still, hot morning. In the scrub above our house some kind of desert bird was making a raspy sound appropriate to the desert.

Lou Buckman was the first to arrive. She pulled up in front of our house in a stripped-down yellow jeep with no top and no doors. She got out of the jeep wearing a big hat and riding clothes. A single blond braid showed below the hat, and her makeup worked beautifully with her face. Her eyes were very big and the color of morning glories. We were arrayed in a friendly manner, on the front porch, and if she found us daunting, she didn't show it.

"Good morning," she said.

"Good morning."

I introduced her to the other men.

Bernard J. Fortunato said, "I got coffee. You want some?"

"Yes, thank you," Lou said. "That would be lovely."

Bernard hustled off as if he were going for the Holy Grail. Lou stood on the porch and looked at us.

"There aren't very many of you," she said.

"But what there is is cherce," Hawk said.

"Cherce?"

"Choice," I said. "It's a line Spencer Tracy used about Katherine Hepburn."

"Oh."

Lou still looked at us.

"You do look dangerous," she said.

"Señorita," Chollo said, "that is because, as we say in my country, we are dangerous."

"What is your country?" Lou said.

Chollo grinned at her.

"Los Angeles," he said.

Lou leaned her admirable little butt on the railing of the porch. Bernard came back and gave her coffee. She thanked him and held the mug in both hands and sipped. Behind her a Ford Expedition pulled into the yard and a Dodge Van, and a big Chrysler Sedan. Our employers got out, warily, as if it might be an ambush, and gathered uneasily in front of the porch. J. George was there on the left looking prosperous and affable. In fact all four of them looked prosperous, and they bore with them the aroma of self-satisfaction that prosperity brings. The mayor stood next to J. George, then Barnes the lawyer and Brown the banker. I stood beside Lou Buckman on the top step of the porch facing them. My posse was ranged along the back wall of the porch, seated, most of them teetering their chairs back so that the front legs cleared the floor.

I looked down at the group. I felt a little like Mussolini. Maybe I should have folded my arms.

"Me you know," I said. "From my right, Hawk, Vinnie Morris, Chollo, Bobby Horse, Tedy Sapp and Bernard J. Fortunato."

The quartet looked as if they thought that the preacher and his crew might be preferable. Luther Barnes spoke first.

"Could we have full names, please?" he said.

"Certainly," I said. "Hawk, your full name, please?"

"Hawk."

"Thank you. Chollo?"

"Chollo."

"Thank you."

Barnes was not amused.

"I just think we have a right to know who we're paying all this money to," he said.

"You're paying it to me," I said.

Roscoe, wearing a panama hat, probably felt the need to say something official sounding.

"I feel there should be some legal foundation for this venture," he said.

I stared at him.

"This group has no legal foundation. It's a group of professional thugs, hired by you."

The group was quiet.

Then Henry Brown said, "I'm a business man, and, a goddamned good one. In all the years of business I never hired a man I didn't know his background."

"Good for you," I said.

"Damn it," he said, "that's no answer."

Sitting on the porch, Chollo took out a handgun and casually shot a small branch off a tree to my right. He did it again, and then again, chopping the branch back further with each shot.

"I am a simple peasant, señor," Chollo said in his stage Mexican accent. "That is all I have for background."

The gunshots lingered, resonating in the hard dry heat. Our employers looked at the tree limb. When they looked back at Chollo the gun was out of sight. Chollo smiled pleasantly. No one had anything to say for a time until the successful businessman spoke again, somewhat more softly.

"They won't know we're involved, will they?"

"They probably will," I said. "They seem to know a lot."

"But might they retaliate?"

"We'll protect you," I said.

"Seven of you?"

"Not all of us at once," I said. "We try to be fair."

Luther said, "I don't think you realize how serious this is."

I snapped.

"Goddamn it, you hired a bunch of thugs to come out and protect you, and we get here, and good heavens, we seem to be thugs, and now you're all in a goddamned twidget about it. You can let us find out who killed Lou Buckman's husband, and clean out the Dell, or you can live with what you've got. We'll just find out who killed her husband. And go home."

"I can't pay all of you," Lou Buckman said.

Hawk grinned at her.

"No charge," he said, and looked at the other men.

Vinnie nodded first. Then Chollo nodded, and Bobby Horse,

and Sapp, and, after a pause, while I could almost see him thinking it over, Bernard J. Fortunato.

"So," I said, "there it is. You want us to clean up the Dell say
so. You don't, beat it."

"If you stay and help her they'll think we are involved anyway," Luther said. "They know everything that goes on in this
town. They probably know we're here."

"Not my problem," I said.

"Unless we pay you."

"Like you told me you would," I said.

The attorney turned to his associates. I thought that the level
of self-satisfaction in the group had declined a bit.

"He's got us over a barrel," the lawyer said. "We'll have to pay
him."

The mayor said, "Another way to put that, I suppose, is that
we are living up to our end of the deal."

"Whatever," Luther said brusquely. "I'm good for my share."

"The bank is prepared to pay you, as well," Brown said.

No one spoke. I looked back at my crew. They showed nothing.

Then Tedy Sapp said, "There goes the Dell."

chapter
39

LATE IN THE afternoon, I sat in Dean Walker's office, enjoying the a/c. One of his patrol cops was at a desk up front doing paper work, with a translucent Bic ballpoint."

"You know the Dell collects protection money from town businesses," I said.

"Know it, yes; prove it, no."

"Do they have a regular collection schedule?"

"Every Thursday."

"So why not catch them doing it and bust them?"

The patrol cop stopped writing for a moment, then continued.

"Several reasons," Walker said.

He had his feet up on the corner of his desk, dark leather cowboy boots gleaming in the sun that filtered in through the tinted windows in the front.

"One," Walker said. "They do it privately, in somebody's office with the door closed. Two, even if I arrested somebody, there'd be no witnesses, and I couldn't hold them. Three, there's forty of them and five of us."

I nodded.

"I didn't know you knew Lou Buckman from L.A.," I said.

Walker didn't register anything, but he took a moment to answer.

"You've been investigating," he said.

"You lived in her neighborhood."

"I did," Walker said.

"And you were a cop there," I said.

"Un-huh."

"L.A. or Santa Monica?"

"L.A. I was a detective. Ramparts Division."

"So how'd you end up here?" I said.

Walker shrugged.

"It was time to stop being a big city cop," he said. "Hell it was time to stop being a cop altogether, but I didn't know how to do anything else."

"Well at least you've reduced the scale," I said. "The Buckmans have anything to do with you coming here?"

"They had a little business out here, summers. They mentioned there was an opening."

"Perfect," I said. "Did they mention the Dell?"

"When I took this job the Dell was just a bunch of stumble-bums squatting in the old mining shacks. They didn't turn into a problem until The Preacher showed up."

"You happen to remember Lou Buckman's maiden name?" I said.

"Allard," he said. "Mary Lou Allard."

"Nice woman," I said.

He nodded.

"Nice woman."

"You know Mark Ratliff in L.A., too?"

"Yep."

"You know how he ended up here in the same town as two of his neighbors in Santa Monica?"

"Must have heard about it from Lou and Steve," Walker said. "Like me."

"And he wanted to get out of the Hollywood rat race?" I said.

Walker smiled.

"He was trailing the other rats by considerable," Walker said.

"What kind of guy is he?"

Walker shrugged again.

"Hollywood guy," Walker said.

"I heard he had a fling with Lou."

Walker's face hardened. I could see the lines deepen on either side of his mouth.

"That's a fucking lie," he said.

I nodded.

"The best kind," I said.

"He was shagging around after her at a couple of parties we went to. But she brushed him off. Stevie was going to punch his lights out."

"We?"

"We what?"

"You said 'we' went to a couple of parties. You married?"

"Divorced."

"Grounds?" I said.

"She knows, and I know," Walker said. "You don't need to."

"What is your ex-wife's name?" I said.

"Same answer."

I nodded

"When you've got one that works, may as well stay with it."

"I'm sick of talking to you, pal," Walker said. "Beat it."

Arguing with him about that didn't lead anywhere. The patrol cop was still concentrating on his report sheet so hard that I wondered, as I left, whether it might begin to smolder.

chapter
40

I WENT BACK TO the house. On the front porch Hawk and Tedy Sapp were doing push-ups. It looked like an interesting contest, since both of them appeared able to do push-ups forever.

Bernard J. Fortunato had drinks set up on the table on the porch. There was Scotch and vodka and soda and tonic, a cooking pot full of ice, and some lemons sliced in wedges and a large soup bowl of peanuts. There were no napkins, but he had put out a number of neatly folded paper towels. Vinnie was drinking Scotch on the rocks. Chollo and Bobby Horse each had vodka and tonic.

"This is taking too long," Hawk said.

He and Sapp looked at each other and grinned and stood up at the same time.

"Not bad," I said to Tedy. "Not many people can stay with Hawk."

"Not good, either," Sapp said. "Nobody ever stayed with me before."

Sapp made a couple of Scotch and sodas and handed one to Hawk. I went in and got a can of beer and came out and sat on the porch railing with one foot hanging free.

"Chollo and Bobby Horse went off somewhere in the car," Bernard reported.

I looked at Chollo.

"I went up and reconnoitered the Dell," Chollo said, "with my faithful Indian companion."

"How'd it look?" I said.

"Hard to get to," Chollo said.

"I know."

"And they got sentries out all night."

"I assume you weren't spotted?"

"Spotted? Señor, I was with the great Kiowa scout, He-who-walks-everywhere-and-is-never-spotted."

Bobby Horse had no reaction. It was as if he didn't hear us.

"Silly question," I said.

"I maybe found a way to get above them and shoot down."

"Can you find it again?" I said.

Bobby Horse drank some vodka and tonic.

"I am a Native American," he said.

"Oh, yeah," I said. "I forgot. Can you show me?"

"If you can walk as softly as I can," Bobby Horse said.

He never smiled. I never knew for sure how much of his white-man-speakum-with-forked-tongue Indian routine was schtick. I was pretty sure most of it was. I looked at his bare chest.

"Tomorrow you can take me and Hawk up there," I said.

He nodded. His upper body was bunched with muscle. There

was a white scar that ran across the coppery skin of his chest, from near the left shoulder almost to his bottom rib on the right side.

"You been out all day with no shirt?" I said.

He nodded again.

"Don't Native Americans get sunburned?" I said.

"Use 'um sunblock."

chapter
41

IN THE MORNING I called Fresno State University and said I was planning to hire Mary Lou Allard, and asked about her undergraduate career. The registrar spoke with enough accent for me to know that English was her second language.

"Ms. Allard graduated cum laude with a Bachelor of Science degree in Geology," she said.

"Date?"

"June 3, 1985."

"Is there anything else you can tell me about her?" I said.

"No sir, there is not."

"Thanks anyway," I said.

. I then called information and asked for Walker in Santa Monica. My question was too hard for the electronic apparatus to which I had asked it, and after a few clicks and bleeps I got a live female voice.

"What listing, please?"

"Judy Walker in Santa Monica," I said.

"What state please?"

"California."

"Do you have a street address?"

"No."

There was a moment of silence in which I knew I was being disapproved of.

Then she said, "One moment, please."

A mechanical voice came back on and gave me a telephone number. I broke the connection and dialed the number. She answered on the third ring.

"My name is Spenser," I said. "I'm a detective working on a case out here in the desert. I understand that your ex-husband is the chief of police in Potshot."

"My ex-husband? Yes, I guess he is. I haven't seen him for nine years."

"I'm doing a little background check. You're divorced from Chief Walker?"

"Yes."

"What were the grounds?" I said.

"Why on earth would you want to know that?"

I laughed.

"Good question," I said. "I guess because my boss will fire me if I don't find out."

She laughed very slightly on her end of the phone.

"We were divorced on the grounds that he coveted his neighbor's wife."

"Really," I said. "And what was her name, if you remember."

"I remember," she said.

"Of course."

She was silent. I waited.

"Mary Lou," she said. "Mary Lou Buckman."

"I see," I said, just like I didn't know. "And, I'm sorry to be so indelicate. But I have to ask. Was his covetousness, ah, fulfilled?"

"You mean was he shacking up with her? Yes."

"You're sure?"

"Of course, I'm sure. That's why I divorced the bastard."

"And I certainly don't blame you," I said. Sincere as a siding salesman. "Do you know where Ms. Buckman is now?"

"Sure. She's out there in Potshot. The dumb bastard followed her out there."

"Are they together?" I said.

She was warm on the subject now and I didn't have to be so delicate. Pretty soon I'd have trouble getting her to shut up.

"Together? No. Of course not. She's married and with her husband. My stupid husband just followed her out there, in case she decided to cheat on her husband again."

"And if she didn't?"

"He could just moon around her, like a big fruit fly. Men are idiots."

"True," I said. "That's so true."

"Her husband even threatened Dean, once, told him to stay away from his wife."

"How did your husband react?"

"Oh he's a policeman, thinks he's a tough guy, like they all do. I think they're a bunch of babies."

"Did they actually have a fight or anything?"

"Not while I was around."

"Did either of them threaten to kill the other?"

"Kill? Oh God no, it wasn't like that. I never said anything about killing. Why are you talking about killing?"

"Just routine, m'am."

"Is Dean all right?" she said.

"He's fine, m'am. Fine."

"Well, is that all? I've got a lot of things waiting for me."

"Yes, m'am. Thank you for your time."

She hung up without saying "you're welcome."

Since I was on a hot streak I called the Department of Water and Power in L.A. and talked with a guy in the personnel department.

"I'm interviewing a Mary Lou Buckman," I said, "for a job. Her resumé says she worked for you. Could you verify that for me?"

"Did she say what section?"

"No."

"Give me a minute," he said.

It was more like ten, but finally he came back on the line.

"I hate computers," he said.

"Any decent person would," I said. "Did you locate Mary Lou Buckman?"

"Yes. She was employed with us from 1986 until 1991."

"In what capacity?"

"Resource development."

"Which means?"

"She was a geologist. She looked for new sources of water."

chapter
42

Hawk and I were looking at the guns laid out in the dining room, where Vinnie had affectionately arranged them. There were two AR-15s, three pump-action shotguns, a Winchester .45 carbine, a Heckler & Koch with a 20-round magazine, a Jaeger Hunter with a scope, a .44 Rugar bush gun, and a BAR.

"Who owns the BAR?" I said.

"Bobby Horse," Vinnie said.

"Bonnie and Clyde use those," Hawk said.

"Don't know nothing about Bonnie and Whosis," Vinnie said.

There were extra handguns on the side board: a Walther P38, two Brownings, a Glock 17, and three Smith & Wesson .357 revolvers. The ammunition for each weapon was stacked beside it. Most of the guns were stainless steel and they gleamed happily in their orderly arrangement. The ammunition boxes were mostly green, or red, depending on who made them. The room looked sort of festive.

"Who brought lever action?" Vinnie said.

"Me," I said. "A sentimental favorite."

Vinnie shook his head and went on wiping.

On the floor in front of a side window two pieces of duct tape formed a large X.

"Firing position?" I said.

"Yeah," Vinnie said. "Got five positions marked. Give us a fields of fire cover the whole house. Got some other positions located up in the hills, case we want to bail out of here, cover any approach."

I nodded.

"How come you got that Winchester?" Vinnie said.

"Sentimental," I said. "I had it in Laramie. My uncle bought it for me."

"You only got five shots in the sucker, and you got to jack each one up before you shoot."

"I'm not big for volume," I said. "I'm a careful shooter."

"Well I hope you ain't feeding shells into that thing while one of the Dell monsters comes at you with a Tec-nine."

"Me too," I said.

"What are packing for a handgun?" Vinnie said.

I pulled my T-shirt up to show him the gun on my belt.

"Same thing," Vinnie said. "Two-inch barrel, five rounds in the cylinder."

"Sometimes I carry that Browning," I said.

"You should," Vinnie said. "You can't hit a whale in the ass with that little Smith & Wesson, unless you're right up on him."

"I plan to be right up," I said.

Vinnie shrugged. I was beginning to feel defensive.

"I like it," I said. "It'll knock you down if you're close. It's light to carry, easy to conceal, and it works good. I can carry it in an ankle holster if I need to."

Vinnie nodded again. With a small camel-hair brush, he was dusting the rear sight of the BAR.

"Besides," I said, "it's cute."

"Yeah, sure," Vinnie said. "And it matches your tie. Swell."

Vinnie's full attention went back to tending the guns. He was like a bitch grooming a puppy.

"Bobby Horse waiting on us," Hawk said, "to go look at the Dell."

"Chollo's not going?"

"Chollo say he already been there."

"Doesn't want to make the climb again," I said.

Hawk nodded. We were quiet for a time watching Vinnie fuss over the weapons.

"There's a lot going on here that we don't know about," I said.

"We used to that," Hawk said.

"And the damn woman is at the center of it."

"We sort of used to that too, ain't we?"

"Yeah but she's also our employer."

"She your employer, Bobo. You're my employer."

"You're such a stickler," I said.

"Chain of command, boss."

Vinnie had the cylinder open on one of the .357s and was studying it, using his thumbnail to reflect light into the barrel. Then he nodded to himself and gently closed the cylinder.

"Vinnie should have been a father," Hawk said.

We watched Vinnie for a minute.

"Something bothering me," Hawk said.

"Only something?"

"Mary Lou and her hubby come out here on their summers off and run this little horseback gig," Hawk said.

"Until he got fired from coaching," I said. "Then they moved out here full-time."

"Who the fuck gonna come out here for summer vacation?" I nodded.

"That is bothersome," I said. "Maybe it was because that's the only time they had off."

"Maybe," Hawk said.

"Or not," I said. "And why here?"

"Maybe you and me need to figure out what's up out here, 'fore we charge up to the Dell and shoot everybody's ass?"

"What's the most important thing in the desert?" I said.

"Iron Horse Champagne," Hawk said.

"Next to that," I said.

"Water."

"Our client was a geologist whose job it was to find new water sources."

"And she was boffing the chief of police."

"Yep."

"And Ratliff the producer."

"Yep."

"And she had enough money to hire you to find out who clipped her hubby."

"And they all come from L.A.," I said.

"Where some bad man tries to chase you off the case."

"And back in Potshot, I prevail over a couple of stiffs from the Dell, and the town fathers treat me like Charlemagne."

Vinnie had the magazine out of the BAR and was feeding shells into it.

"Costing a lot of money," Hawk said. "Support you and me and five tough guys."

"They could get the Sheriff's Department to clean out the Dell for zip," I said.

" 'Cept they afraid to testify."

"So why aren't they afraid to hire us? You think the Dell won't know?"

"So maybe they ain't so scared," Hawk said.

"Or maybe they are," I said. "But there's something at stake that's worth the risk."

"Which they couldn't get if the cops came in," Hawk said.

Vinnie put the full clip back in the BAR, worked the action once, caught the ejected shell in midair, took the magazine out, and reloaded the shell.

"Works good," he said.

chapter
43

BOBBY HORSE TOOK Hawk and me slowly up the back slope of the hill behind the Dell. It was steep and littered with shale and spiky with dry desert growth. We took two and a half hours to get to the top and another half-hour to reach the rim where the hill dropped off perpendicularly and formed the back wall of the Dell.

Flat on our stomachs, screened by the scrub growth that hung onto the canyon, we could see the Quonset huts of The Preacher's crew directly below us, and beyond, where the canyon dropped off again as it stepped down toward the desert, the town clustered on the otherwise empty flat land. To our left was the ravine that led into the canyon, through which I came to visit The Preacher. It was the only way in, which made the place secure. It was also the only way out.

"Hard to go in there," Hawk said.

I said, "Un-huh."

"Hard to get out of there."

"Un-huh."

The heavy dry heat was battering. Sweat dried at once.

"Dumb," Hawk said. "All they saw was how hard it was to get in."

"They didn't choose the site," I said. "It was just sort of there, where the mine was, and I don't think they ever thought they'd have to get out."

"Probably didn't think there'd be anyone willing to make the fucking climb," Hawk said to me. "You be the only one I can think of."

Bobby Horse passed around a big canteen and we all drank some water. The water was hot.

"It's not boiling," I said, "so the temperature must be less than 212."

"What temperature you suppose ammunition start exploding?" Hawk said.

We were all silent, staring down at the Dell.

"Put some people up here," Bobby Horse said, "and some people at the ravine down there and we can shoot them to pieces."

I was going to say something about fish in a barrel, but the imagery didn't seem quite right for the parched furnace below us.

"We'll keep it in mind," I said.

"Why not just do it?" Bobby Horse said.

"He too sweet-natured," Hawk said to Bobby Horse.

"Besides," I said, "means we'd have to climb down, get people together, and climb back up here with rifles."

"I be one of the folks at the ravine," Hawk said.

"If it comes to that we'll draw straws," I said. "Except me. As you pointed out, I'm your employer."

"I believe you discriminating racially," Hawk said, " 'gainst me and my Native American sidekick."

"You were the one said we needed to know more before we started shooting," I said.

"I didn't mean it," Hawk said.

Bobby Horse paid no attention to us, as he stared down at the Dell.

"Looks like a generator shack over there," he said.

"Yes, I said. "You can see the hookups to the other buildings."

"Where's the fuel?" Hawk said.

"Barrels," Bobby Horse said. "Other side of the building. They set one on a high stand and run a hose into the generator. Works on gravity."

"You got a look at the other side?" Hawk said.

"Me and Chollo," Bobby Horse said. "We went over to that little jut at the end of the canyon."

"No wonder Chollo didn't want to come again," I said.

"Mexicans tire easy," Bobby Horse said.

We looked at the Dell some more. There was a large stake body truck parked near the generator shack. It was probably used to haul the fuel oil.

"Might be good to take that generator out," Bobby Horse said. "No lights, no television, no a/c."

"Water be pumped up from a well," Hawk said. "So no running water."

"How we going to take it out?"

"I go down," Bobby Horse said.

"You could get down there?"

"Sure."

"And back?"

"Sure."

"We'll keep it in mind," I said.

We lay for awhile baking at the top of the cliff looking at the Dell.

"When I went in to talk to The Preacher, when I was here before, nobody stopped me. I didn't see any sentries."

Bobby Horse pointed toward the ravine. Hawk and I looked. I saw nothing.

"Keep looking," Bobby Horse said. "Near the top of the ravine. A cluster of scrub? Just below it a ledge? Under the ledge."

I found the scrub and the ledge and kept looking. Then I saw a glint of light reflecting from under the ledge."

"Gun barrel," Bobby Horse said, "belt buckle, sunglasses, maybe a wristwatch."

"How many you think?" I said.

"Two," Bobby Horse said.

There was no uncertainty in his voice.

"So they let me in because I was alone and not carrying any visible weapons," I said.

"Probably thought you was a tourist got lost," Bobby Horse said.

"Or a dashing soldier of fortune," I said. "And they hoped to recruit me."

"We put somebody at the ravine," Hawk said, "we need to eliminate them first."

"I can do that," Bobby Horse said.

"Both of them?" I said.

"Sure."

"You Native Americans are scary," Hawk said.

"Heap scary," Bobby Horse said.

"Talk funny, too." I said.

We stayed on our bellies and stared down through the shimmering that rose from the canyon floor, until most of our water was gone, and we had internalized the layout of the Dell. Then we edged away from the rim, stood and walked the half-hour walk back to the down slope of the hill behind the Dell.

"We got the people to do this," Hawk said as we started the long scramble back down. "You put the shooters up here, Vinnie, Chollo, maybe the little hard case from Vegas. Me and you do the close work in the ravine, with Tedy Sapp and Bobby Horse."

"If we need to," I said.

"How you going to know if we need to?"

"When I figure out what's happening here. I'm not going to slaughter a bunch of people and then find out we didn't have to."

Hawk shook his head slowly.

"A sweet nature," he said. "A sweet fucking nature."

chapter
44

W HEN WE GOT back to the house there was a silver Lexus parked in front and Chollo was sitting on the front porch with Morris Tannenbaum's guy with the horn-rimmed glasses, who looked like an accountant but wasn't.

"You remember Ronnie," Chollo said.

"With pleasure," I said.

Bobby Horse paid no attention to Ronnie. He went on past him and into the house. Hawk didn't say anything but he looked steadily at Ronnie. Ronnie looked at Hawk for a time and then turned his attention to me. Hawk leaned against the porch railing, still looking at Ronnie.

"Hot," Ronnie said.

He was wearing a white linen suit with a flowered sport shirt open at the neck. His shoes were woven leather. He looked like an accountant on vacation.

"Yeah," I said, "but it's a dry heat."

Ronnie nodded as if the heat were a real topic. I waited.

"Morris wanted me to talk with you," Ronnie said.

"You always do what Morris wants?" I said.

"Yeah."

I waited some more. Ronnie seemed in no hurry. Hawk was motionless against the railing. Chollo might have been asleep in his chair.

"Morris wanted me to tell you things have changed a little," Ronnie said.

"Un-huh."

"Morris says he got no further interests out here."

"Which means?"

"Morris says if you want to take out the Dell, he'll give you a walk on that."

"Last I knew he was going to have somebody shoot me if I didn't leave things alone out here."

"Probably me," Ronnie said. "That ain't the case anymore."

"Well isn't that nice," I said. "How about Mary Lou Buckman?"

"Morris got no interest in her."

"But he used to," I said.

Ronnie spread his hands, palms up, and shrugged.

"What happened?" I said.

Ronnie shook his head.

"Morris didn't have anybody shoot Steve Buckman did he?"

"Nope."

"You sure?"

"I do Morris's shooting," Ronnie said. "I didn't do Buckman."

"You know who did?"

"Maybe she did," Ronnie said.

"Why do you think so?"

"Wives shoot husbands a lot," Ronnie said.

"What's Morris's connection to her?"

"Maybe they were bridge partners. Morris only tells me what I need to know."

"And his connection to the Dell?"

"Same answer," Ronnie said.

"So Morris sent you all the way out here just to tell me it was okay to do what I was going to do anyway?" I said.

"We had no way to know you was going to do it," Ronnie said.

"What the hell was I doing here, then?"

"Maybe shagging after Mrs. Buckman," Ronnie said.

"With half a dozen thugs?"

Ronnie smiled. It was a thin gesture, but unexpected.

"Maybe to hold her down?" he said.

"I'll be damned, a romantic underneath it all."

Ronnie hitched up a pant leg, and crossed his right leg over his left. He bobbed his right foot a little, looking at the toe of his shoe as if it were interesting.

"Morris says he'd like to make a financial contribution to the project," Ronnie said.

"Which project is that?" I said.

"Snuffing the Dell."

"How about Mary Lou?"

"Leave her on her own."

"You mean don't look after her?" I said.

"Let things develop," he said. "Stay focused on the Dell."

"How much of a financial contribution is Morris likely to make?" I said.

"You could pretty much name it," Ronnie said. "If you can deliver."

"But no manpower," I said.

"Nope."

"Why not?"

"Morris figures you don't need it."

"How flattering," I said.

"Chollo and Bobby Horse are good," Ronnie said.

"You are too kind, señor," Chollo said.

Ronnie nodded at Hawk.

"This guy's good," he said.

Hawk registered nothing.

"You can tell?" I said.

"I can tell," Ronnie said. "You too."

"You know anything about Dean Walker?"

"Police chief out here, isn't he?"

"Know more than that?"

"Nope."

"How do you know that?"

"I'm alert," Ronnie said.

"What about Mark Ratliff?"

"Movie producer," Ronnie said, "except he don't produce no movies."

"Anything else?"

"Nope."

"And how do you know about him?"

Ronnie smiled the thin smile again.

"Alertness," he said.

"I'm pretty alert myself," I said. "And I notice that Morris is hiring me to do what he said he'd kill me for a month ago."

"Things change," Ronnie said.

"But you wouldn't know why?"

"I wouldn't," Ronnie said. "Like I said, Morris only tells me what he thinks I need to know."

"Why don't I believe you?" I said.

"Because you're a cynical and suspicious guy?" Ronnie said.

"That must be it," I said.

We sat. Hawk leaned. I tried to think of some clever way to trick Ronnie into telling more than he wanted to. I couldn't. I was cynical and suspicious, but not that bright.

"Tell Morris that I will decline his kind offer, and if anything happens to Mary Lou Buckman I will come to L.A. and fry his ass."

"I'll pass that on," Ronnie said.

He got up and headed for his car. Hawk watched him all the way. Chollo didn't move but I realized he was watching Ronnie too. Ronnie went around his car and opened the driver's-side door. He looked back at us.

"Have a nice day," he said.

Then he got in the car and closed the door and backed it slowly out of the driveway.

chapter
45

It was Bernard's turn to cook breakfast. He valued presentation. He always put out a tablecloth and matching flatware. He put the juice in a pitcher and the milk in another. No cartons on the table. He served the meals from the counter instead of slopping the food out of the cooking pan at the table. Today he was serving apricot pancakes with syrup made from some sort of cactus pear.

"Bernard," Tedy Sapp said, "you sure you're straight?"

"Damned right I'm straight," Bernard said. "Anybody says I'm not I'll fight him."

Sapp grinned.

"When a gay guy calls you queer, it's not an insult," he said.

"You think I wouldn't fight you?" Bernard said.

"I think you would," Sapp said. "Just not for long."

Bernard put three pancakes on a dinner plate and brought it to the table.

"Well you just mess with me," he said. "We'll find out how long."

Sapp's grin grew wider.

He said, "I wouldn't mess with you Bernard."

Bernard put my pancakes down in front of me. They were carefully arranged on the plate so that they didn't overlap. I put just enough honey on and cut off a bite and ate it.

When I had swallowed, I said, "You can really cook for a straight guy Bernard."

"Don't you start with me," he said.

"Why would Morris Tannenbaum send Ronnie here?" Chollo said.

"I figure he got double-crossed," I said.

"By who?"

"Everybody involved."

"Which is who?" Hawk said.

"I'll get back to you on that," I said.

"He has many resources," Chollo said. "Why not send Ronnie and some people out here, straighten it out himself?"

"Why," I said, "if we'll do it for him?"

"Why does he wish to pay us for something we're going to do even if he does not?"

I looked at Hawk.

" 'Cause he been double-crossed," Hawk said. "And he can't let no one do that and get off. So he wants it to be him paid us."

Chollo looked at me. I nodded.

"Be my guess," I said.

"You have not ever met the man."

"Magical, ain't it?" Hawk said.

"So why not permit him to pay us?" Chollo said.

"Step at a time," I said. "First let's shove The Preacher a little."

"About time," Vinnie murmured.

Hawk looked at him. Vinnie shrugged and didn't say more. Vinnie looked up to Hawk.

"We going to go in after them?" Chollo said.

"Not yet," I said. "We interfere with their ability to do business, see what it brings us."

"You think you can get them to bargain?" Sapp said.

"He thinks he can get them to tell him who killed Buckman."

"He does?" Sapp said.

"That how he is," Hawk said.

Bernard came from the counter with his own plate of pancakes and sat down. He tucked his napkin into his collar, and picked up his knife and fork.

"Why's he care who killed Buckman?" Bernard said.

"Hawk's right," Chollo said. "I worked with him before, what was the name of that place where we found the broad?"

"Proctor," I said.

"Yeah, Proctor," Chollo said. "Up outside Boston. When I was up there with him, he worried about things that the rest of us don't worry so much about."

Chollo looked at Sapp.

" 'Cept maybe him," he said.

"That's a mean thing to say to me," Sapp said.

"Today's Wednesday," I said. "The Preacher and his associates come in to town on Thursday and collect money from the town."

"You going to brace them then?" Sapp said.

"He won't do nothing that simple," Vinnie said.

"We're going to watch them," I said. "See who they collect from, and when. Then we look around town and figure out, knowing the collection pattern, we see if we can develop a game plan, which does not involve shooting a bunch of civilians while we're bracing them."

"See?" Vinnie said.

Bobby Horse had said nothing, eating six pancakes in the process. Now he looked up.

"Good plan," he said.

"Might make sense," Hawk said. "We go in today, look around."

I had just poured a second cup of coffee. I added milk and a lot of sugar and stirred it carefully.

"It would," I said. "But not as a group. Just drift in individually, maybe couple guys together."

"I'll go in with Tedy," Bernard said.

"I'd be honored," Sapp said.

"What you going to do?" Hawk said.

"How do you know he's not going to go in with us?" Bernard said.

Hawk smiled and didn't answer.

"I'm going to go and talk with Mary Lou."

" 'Bout time," Hawk said.

"It is," I said.

chapter
46

THE RATTLESNAKE CAFE was long and narrow with an open kitchen to the right and high-back wooden booths along the left wall. The ceiling was tin. The booths were painted with desert scenes. The tabletops were Mexican tile.

Mary Lou Buckman and I sat in the first booth, and I, mindful of Wild Bill Hickok, sat facing the door. We were reading the menus. Among the choices were a chicken breast sandwich on sourdough bread with sprouts; blackened salmon; a Desert Burger with green chili relish; and a Cactus Club Sandwich.

Bernard J. Fortunato's apricot pancakes were sticking grimly to my ribs, and, an oddity for me, I wasn't very hungry. Mary Lou decided on the Desert Burger. I ordered the Cactus Club, to be sociable. We both had iced tea.

"What is the occasion for this lunch?" Mary Lou said. "Not, of course, that I'm not thrilled to see you."

She was wearing a white baseball cap, the kind where you can adjust the size by moving a plastic strap in the back. Her blond hair was spooled through the adjustment opening and hung in a long braid to her shoulders. Her dark blue tank top revealed a little self-effacing cleavage, and I had noticed when she walked in that her white shorts were well fitted.

"That would be one reason," I said. "The other is that I'm your employee. It seems appropriate for me to report to you now and then."

She had applied her makeup so adroitly that she looked as if she wore none, except her eyes were bigger and her lashes were thicker than God had intended. She still smelled of good soap, and her tan was still even. Except for the plain gold wedding ring on her left hand, she wore no jewelry. *In memoriam.*

The food arrived. The Cactus Club contained chicken, tomato, bacon, and lettuce, but no cactus.

"Very well," she said, and smiled a little, "report."

"I've been to L.A.," I said.

She had a bite of Desert Burger in her mouth. She raised her eyebrows and said nothing.

"There are several people there who allege that both you and your husband fooled around."

She blushed. It had been so long since I had seen someone blush that it took me a moment to be sure what she was doing. She swallowed, and took her napkin from her lap, and patted her mouth with it, and put the napkin back in her lap.

"Steve and I had an open marriage," she said.

"People allege that a couple of the people you fooled around with are Mark Ratliff and Dean Walker."

She stared at me without speaking for a time.

I waited.

Finally she said, "Why do you feel the need to investigate my private life?"

"It's what I do," I said. "I investigate stuff."

"It is not what you were hired to do."

"While I was in L.A. a big old ugly hoodlum warned me to stay away from you or he'd kill me."

"My God."

"He also told me to stay away from the Dell."

Mary Lou seemed to have forgotten her Desert Burger.

"What does this all mean?" she said.

"It means that a guy who pretty much runs the rackets east of L.A. is interested in you and the Dell. It means that two men, at least, who knew you, ah, intimately, appear to have followed you out here."

"They didn't follow me."

I nodded.

"I never had anything to do with either one of them."

"Guy who warned me off is named Morris Tannenbaum," I said.

"I never heard of him," she said. "I don't know what all this is about."

"I'm just reporting," I said. "And this is what I've got to report."

"Well it doesn't feel that way," she said. "It feels like you are accusing me."

"Of what?"

"I don't know of what. Do you think I killed my husband?"

"It would have been sensible, when you hired me to look into his death, if you'd told me a little more about your past and its connection to your present," I said.

"I don't even know what that means," she said.

She seemed like she might cry soon.

"I'm alone here. A gang of thugs killed my husband. I turned to you for help. I had nowhere else to turn."

"What do you suppose is out here that would interest Morris Tannenbaum?" I said.

"Who?"

"The racketeer," I said. "Remember?"

"Oh. Yes."

"What would be his interest?"

"I can't imagine."

"You worked once for the DWP in L.A.," I said.

She stared silently ahead, not making eye contact. Then she began to moan softly.

"I wanted you to help me," she said between moans. "Why won't you help me?"

"You had a job in water resource," I said.

"I can't do this," she said. "I can't."

She stood up and walked out.

chapter
47

IT WAS COOLER once the sun went down. Hawk and I sat on the front porch of The Jack Rabbit Inn drinking Coors beer from long-neck bottles, and looking at the darkening street.

"So Mary Lou told you shit," Hawk said.

"She told me I was the only one who could help her," I said.

"Probably the first guy she ever said that to."

Hawk was wearing faded blue jeans and a copper-colored silk tweed jacket over a white shirt. His mahogany-colored cowboy boots gleamed with polish. Everything fit him flawlessly. I knew that he was wearing his gun at the small of his back so as not to break the drape.

"I'm very special to her," I said.

"Un-huh. She say anything about Walker and Ratliff?"

"She said they weren't intimate."

"We believe her, don't we?" Hawk said.

"There's a lot she isn't saying," I said.

"We knew that 'fore you talked with her," Hawk said.

"Well, we know it again," I said.

"Skilled interrogation be the keystone of detective work," Hawk said.

"Yes it be," I said.

"Snooping around town work pretty well too."

"The Dell came in for collections," I said.

"Un-huh. Two Jeep loads. Actually one a Jeep, the other one an old Scout, don't even make anymore."

"I've seen it," I said. "What time?"

"10:20 in the morning," Hawk said.

"Not early birds," I said.

"Still got themselves a worm though."

"Preacher come with them?"

"Casper the ghost," Hawk said. "Skinny? No hair?"

"That's him."

"He done the collecting," Hawk said. "Started down there, head of the street, at the Western Wear Store, and worked right down Main Street."

"How much backup?"

"Seven, besides him. Four in each vehicle. When he went in the stores, a big fat guy went with him. Carried the black bag."

"Pony," I said.

"Pony?"

"That's his name."

"Guy's big enough to haul a beer wagon."

"Maybe they're being ironic," I said.

"Tha's probably it," Hawk said. "I bet there's a lot of irony out there in the old Dell."

"What'd the other guys do while The Preacher was collecting?"

"Moved along down the street with him," Hawk said. "Stayed in the vehicles while Preacher and Pony went in."

"Weapons?"

"Handguns probably. I didn't see anything bigger."

When Hawk was engaged by something, he occasionally forgot his mocking black accent. It was how you could tell he was engaged.

"This is beginning to sound easy," I said.

"It'll be easy," Hawk said.

"They know we're here," I said.

"Probably. But The Preacher's been the stud horse around here a long time. He's so used to not having trouble that he forgot there is any. My guess, he don't care if we're here."

"You working on a plan?" I said.

Hawk nodded toward the head of the street

"We park Sapp in one car up there," he said. "And we put Bobby Horse in the other car, at the bottom of the street. Chollo in the alley there." Hawk pointed with his chin at a point midway along Main Street. "The little Vegas guy . . ."

"Bernard," I said. "Bernard J. Fortunato."

"Him," Hawk said. "Across and down a little, between the bakery and the drug store. And Vinnie in the hotel window, top floor."

"Why Vinnie?" I said.

"Best shooter," Hawk said.

"I'm not sure he's better than Chollo," I said.

"He ain't worse," Hawk said.

"No. You're right. Vinnie's in the window. Which leaves you and me to brace Pony and The Preacher."

"Best for last," Hawk said and took a pull at his beer.

"Okay," I said. "That'll work."

" 'Course it'll work," Hawk said. "You just jealous you didn't think it up."

"How hard was it to think up?" I said.

"Tha's not the point," Hawk said.

"Of course it isn't," I said. "Next week we'll implement your plan."

"Hot diggity," Hawk said.

chapter 48

J. GEORGE TAYLOR ASKED me to come talk with him. Except for J. George, the office was empty when I got there.

"Mary Lou says you've been questioning her," he said after I was seated in his client chair.

"She does?" I said.

"She feels you were somewhat accusative."

"And she complained to you?"

"We're friends. Since her husband's death, I have been looking out for her, sort of like a father."

"Sort of," I said.

"And I really think she needs a gentle touch. For God's sake, her husband was murdered."

"By the Dell," I said.

"Of course, by the Dell."

"You know this."

"Everyone knew that he was standing up to the Dell. Everyone knew they had threatened him."

"Who did the actual threatening?"

"The Dell."

"Which one?"

"The Preacher."

"You heard him?"

"No. It was his, ah, brute—Pony."

"You heard Pony threaten Steve?"

"Of course. Half the town heard him."

"Who besides you, specifically?"

"Oh, for God's sake," J. George said. "The mayor heard him. Luther Barnes. Mark Ratliff. Henry Brown. About two dozen other people in the bar."

"Which bar?"

"The bar at The Jack Rabbit."

"Tell me about it."

"Nothing to tell," J. George said. "Steve was at the bar, having a beer. Pony walked in and went right up to him and threatened him."

"With death?"

"Yes."

"What did he say?"

"Pony? I don't remember exactly. They had an argument and Steve was shouting, and Pony tapped him on the chest with his forefinger and said to him, 'You're a dead man.' "

"How did Steve react?"

"He just stared at Pony. He wouldn't admit it later, but I think he was scared. Pony is . . . my God, Pony is terrifying."

"I've seen him."

"And?"

"Terrifying," I said.

"But we've gotten off the track," J. George said. "I really wanted to urge you to go easy on Mary Lou."

"You bet," I said. "You know anybody named Morris Tannenbaum?"

J. George leaned back in his chair and looked thoughtful.

"Morris Tannenbaum," he said.

"Yes."

"No. I can't say that I have."

"Spend much time in Los Angeles?" I said.

"No more than I must," J. George said. "Will you be able to give Mary Lou a little more space?"

"Of course," I said. "Sorry I upset her."

J. George stood and put out his hand.

"I know, I know," J. George said. "Just trying to do your job. Women are difficult."

I shook his hand and smiled as if I believed everything he said. Outside I forged bravely through the heat to The Jack Rabbit Inn. Bebe was at a table having lunch with another woman. There were some papers between them. I smiled at Bebe and went to the bar. The bartender came down to me and put a paper doily on the bar in front of me.

"What can I get you?" he said.

"Were you working the bar," I said, "when Pony threatened Steve Buckman?"

"I got nothing to say about that," the bartender said.

"It's just background," I said. "I'll never quote you."

I put a $100 bill on the bar. The bartender looked at it, and then palmed it off the bar in a move so expert that the bill seemed to disappear magically.

"You do and I'll say you're lying."

"Sure," I said.

"Yeah. I was here."

"Tell me about it."

"Steve's at the bar. This monstrous big dude from the Dell comes in. Him and Steve have an argument. The Dude says to Steve, 'You're a dead man.' And walks out."

"The big dude was Pony?"

"Yeah."

The bartender went down the bar and got drink orders from a couple of blonde women in tennis whites. He mixed two cosmopolitans and poured them out into two glasses and it came out just right. He put the drinks in front of the blondes, rang the tab, put it in the bar gutter in front of them, and came back down the bar to me.

"You want something to drink?"

"Sure, give me a Perrier with a slice of orange in it."

"You got it," he said and reached under the bar.

"Ice?"

"Yeah. Lot of people hear him?"

"Pony?"

"Yeah."

"When he threatened Steve Buckman?"

"It's my only hundred," I said.

The bartender grinned.

"Can't blame me for trying," he said. "Sure lot of people heard him. Bar was full. All the regulars."

"J. George?" I said.

"Taylor?" the bartender glanced at Bebe across the room and lowered his voice. "Yeah he was here, and his crew. Barnes, Brown, the mayor."

"Who else?" I said.

"Christ what am I, a computer? Billy Bates was here with his wife. Mr. and Mrs. Gordon. Ratliff the producer. Tom Paglia."

He put my Perrier down on the little doily. I put a ten on the bar. He grinned.

"On the house," he said.

The woman across from Bebe stood up. They shook hands. The woman took some of the papers and left. I moved over to her table as Bebe was sliding the remaining papers into her briefcase. She looked up as I sat down across from her.

"Well, hello," she said.

"Hello."

"I just sold a nice Spanish-style ranch to that woman," Bebe said. "She's from Flagstaff. Sick the snow, I guess."

"How is business these days?"

"Hideous," she said. "Nearly everybody wants to sell, and nobody wants to buy, unless they're from out of town and don't know about the Dell."

"And you don't feel obligated to tell them."

"No, I don't," she said. "Real estate prices are dropping like a stone. They used to be really high, because there was nowhere to expand."

"You're in the middle of nowhere," I said. "Why can't you expand?"

"It's all desert," Bebe said. "We've expanded to the limit of our water supply already."

"What if you had enough water?"

"The Dell would ruin sales anyway."

"What if the Dell were gone?"

Bebe smiled at me.

"I'd be selling real estate as from early in the morning to really late at night," she said.

"Anybody buying property these days?"

"George made a couple of sales to some developer," she said. "I think they'll lose their shirt."

She paused and smiled and shrugged.

"But they're consenting adults," she said.

"Caveat emptor," I said.

The papers were stashed in her little black briefcase. She zipped the top closed and looked up at me from under her eyebrows.

"I was a little fuzzy, the last time I saw you," she said. "I shouldn't drink on a light breakfast."

"None of us should," I said. "But sometimes we do."

"Did we have a good time?" she said.

I tried to put a lecherous gleam in my eyes. It wasn't hard. I was good at lecherous.

"How quickly they forget," I said.

"Was I alright?"

"You certainly were," I said.

I wasn't as good at enthusiasm. But she didn't seem to notice.

"I hate not remembering. Maybe we should go over it again sometime."

"Be my pleasure," I said.

"That's what they tell me," Bebe said.

"Did you know that Mary Lou knew both Dean Walker and Mark Ratliff in Los Angeles?"

"I knew about Mark," Bebe said. "I don't think I knew that about Dean Walker."

"You told me that Mary Lou Buckman was sleeping with both of them."

"And probably some others," Bebe said. "I knew you'd have trouble believing it. Men are so stupid."

"How do you know?"

"About Mary Lou?"

"And Walker and Ratliff," I said.

"Dean Walker is merely surmise," Bebe said, "and intuition."

"And Ratliff?"

Bebe smiled.

"Pillow talk," she said.

I nodded and we smiled knowingly. Two insiders. Intimates.

"You mean I'm not the only one?" I said.

"Almost."

"He say anything else about her?" I said.

"Mark? About Mary Lou? Oh yes. Actually it was a little annoying. He'd be in bed with me. You know, afterwards. And he'd be blabbing on about how he loved Mary Lou and had followed her to Potshot and would wait forever if he had to . . . crap like that."

"You didn't believe him?" I said.

"Mark's a Hollywood person," she said. "It's hard to believe a word he speaks."

"And he wasn't waiting for her celibately," I said.

Bebe was good at lecherous gleaming too.

"Not likely," she said. "But as soon as he was through boffing me, he'd talk about her."

"So, she was always on his mind," I said.

Bebe grinned.

"She was always on his mind."

chapter
49

I CALLED CAWLEY DARK and talked with him for fifteen minutes. Then I hung up and went out onto the front porch where Tedy Sapp was taking orders and mixing drinks. The sun had set, quite flamboyantly, and the blue twilight was settling around us the way it does. Bernard J. Fortunato had fixed up a tray of cheese and crackers and was passing it around.

"Bernard went in today and rented the hotel room," Hawk said. "Street side."

"I told him straight when I reserved it what I wanted," Bernard said.

"You see the room?" I said.

"Bet your ass."

"So Vinnie's in the window with a rifle," Hawk said.

"Room looks right down on the broad's office," Bernard said.

"Mary Lou's?"

"Yeah. Buckman Outfitters."

"So we'll be sure to brace them there," I said. "In front of her storefront."

"You want us to be surreptitious?" Hawk said.

"Surreptitious?" Sapp said.

Hawk shrugged.

"I educated in head start," Hawk said.

"Really worked," Sapp said.

"No reason to be covert," I said.

"You too?" Sapp said.

"Nope," I said. "I'm a straight Anglo white guy of European ancestry. We're naturally smart."

"You missed Bernard," Sapp said.

"*Tall* straight Anglo white guy," I said.

"Hey," Bernard said.

"Perfect," Sapp said.

"So we all got shotguns but Vinnie," Hawk said.

"Sure," I said. "The town fathers hired us to do this. Cops won't interfere."

"You know that?" Vinnie said.

"They haven't so far," I said. "What are you going to use from the window?"

"The Heckler," Vinnie said.

"Good choice," I said.

"Of course it is," Vinnie said.

"I will use a handgun," Chollo said. "Giving me a shotgun is like asking Picasso to paint with a broom."

Vinnie nodded.

"Just what I need," I said. "A couple of divas."

I looked at Bobby Horse.

"I suppose you want a bow and arrow," I said.

"Kiowas are flexible," he said.

We were quiet. Sapp went around refreshing drinks.

"Try the blue cheese," Bernard said. "Nice lingering bite to it."

I looked at Hawk.

"J. George Taylor talked with me today," I said. "Asked me not to annoy Mary Lou."

"Well, then, you better not," Hawk said.

"Then I had a club soda with Bebe Taylor," I said.

"I thought you was going to introduce me," Hawk said.

"I thought you liked a challenge," I said.

"Out here getting laid a challenge," Hawk said.

"She said that it was hard to sell real estate because of the Dell."

"Un-huh."

"She said everybody wants to sell, and nobody wants to buy. Real estate prices are dropping like a stone."

"Sure," Bernard said. "That's the old law of supply and demand. So what?"

Hawk sat back in his chair and put his feet up on the railing. He had a small drink of gin and tonic.

"So the natural price for property here been artificially lowered," he said.

"By the Dell."

"So who benefits from that?" Hawk said.

"Anybody wants to pick up some nice bargains."

Hawk nodded.

"Wouldn't be the Dell," he said.

"They acquire it, the property values won't increase," I said.

"Less they targeting the ex-con market."

"Maybe they don't care about that," Sapp said. "Maybe they just like living off the carcass."

"If the town keeps declining," I said, "there won't be any carcass."

Hawk was nodding his head slowly.

"But if somebody picked up a lot of the real estate, and got rid of the Dell, then they make a big profit."

"She said even if it were good the town couldn't expand because of water limitations."

"But if somebody discovered a new water source?" Hawk said.

"Bonanza," I said.

"What'd Mary Lou Buckman used to do in L.A.?"

"Water resource specialist," I said.

"Fancy that," Hawk said.

chapter
50

I WAS BACK IN Cawley Dark's office with the air-conditioning humming steadily. Dark had on a blue oxford shirt today. With him was a red-haired guy with a big Adam's apple.

"This is Ray Butler," Dark said. "He's the water resource guy for the county."

Butler and I shook hands. We sat in the two chairs facing Dark's desk.

"I told Ray about your situation down in Potshot. He was real impressed that I was doing legwork for a Boston shoo-fly."

"Me too," I said.

Dark leaned back and made a go-ahead gesture at me with his right hand.

"What's the water situation in Potshot?" I said to Butler.

"The Arapaho Aquifer," he said. "Extends from around Salt

City in the Sawtooths, maybe eighty-five miles down through Potshot."

"An aquifer is like an underground river?" I said.

"More like an underground sponge," Butler said. He had a high, sharp voice. "Which holds water, and can be caused to yield it through wells or springs. The water seeps through pores and fractures in consolidated rock, or through spaces between the particles if it's unconsolidated."

"Thank you," I said.

Leaning back in his chair with his fingers laced over his flat stomach, Dark might have been in a reverie, except that there was a hint of amusement in the way his eyes moved.

"There are, of course, confined aquifers and unconfined aquifers."

"Of course," I said. "Is the Arapaho aquifer sufficient to the needs of Potshot?"

"Barely," Butler said.

"Does that limit development?"

"Of course it does," Butler keened.

Talking to the likes of me was clearly painful for him.

"What would happen if the water consumption exceeded the capacity of the aquifer?"

"It could not recharge at a pace sufficient to the need."

Everything Butler said sounded like sort of a high-pitched protest.

"So they'd run out of water."

"That's what I just said."

"Is there any possibility that there is another aquifer?"

"Of course there is. It would be presumptuous to suggest that we know everything about the substrata."

"Presumptuous," I said. "Is it likely?"

Butler paused. How to say this to an unscientific moron?

"It's possible," he said finally.

"And if there were an increase in the amount of available water," I said. "Then I assume it would support increased development."

"It would make it possible," Butler said, "where, right now, it is not."

"Anybody been looking for water down there?"

"No."

"How do you know?"

"In this environment, water is very precious," Butler said. "We cannot permit it to be exploited without supervision."

"So how would you know," I said.

"We'd know."

"How?"

Butler was silent. It was impossible that this rube had asked him a question he couldn't answer.

"Do you know how," I said to Dark.

Dark shook his head.

"There would be evidence of exploration," Butler said.

"When's the last time you looked?"

Again Butler was silent.

After awhile Dark said, "Well thank you very much, Ray, I don't believe we'll be needing anything else."

Butler stood and shook hands with me, sourly, I thought, and departed.

"Ray's never met a man he didn't like," Dark said.

"Be fun to drink beer with," I said.

"If you drank a real lot," Dark said.

"You able to get anyone to check the real estate?"

"Course I did," Dark said. "I'm the goddamned police."

"And?"

"And I had somebody go over to the county hall, like you wanted, and look up real estate transactions in and around Potshot. Here's a list."

Dark handed me the list.

"Recognize any names?" he said.

"Couple," I said. "Who's this Saguaro Development Associates?"

"Thought you'd ask me that," Dark said.

He handed me another sheet.

"Recognize any names?" he said.

"All of them," I said.

I took it and folded it over and tucked it in the inside pocket of my elegant toffee-colored summer silk tweed jacket, which I wore to conceal my somewhat less elegant, blue-barreled handgun.

chapter
51

"WE WALKED THROUGH IT," Hawk said at breakfast. "Without the shotguns."

"Or the Heckler," Vinnie said.

"I have no shotgun," Chollo said.

"Artists are so self-absorbed," I said. "You see anything wrong with the plan?"

"It should be smooth," Hawk said. "Vinnie got a nice view of the street. We do it right we'll be right up against them 'fore they got any idea we there."

"I want to get a look at Pony," Tedy Sapp said.

"Be easy to spot him," Hawk said.

Sapp poured himself more coffee.

"For crissake, Tedy," Bernard said. "How many cups is that?"

"Six."

"Don't you get all jeeped up?" Bernard said.

"Sure," Tedy said. "It's why I drink it."

"You learn anything yesterday worth knowing?" Hawk said to me.

"Potshot can't get any bigger," I said. "Unless there's an additional source of water."

"Like somebody finds an underground river?" Hawk said.

I shook my head pityingly.

"It's a common misconception," I said, "that water flows underground like a river. Most aquifers are better thought of as a giant sponge, which holds the water. One such aquifer, the Arapaho Aquifer, supplies the water currently sustaining Potshot."

"Anglos are generally dull," Chollo said, "but you señor, you are truly so."

"So are there any other underground sponges beside the Arapaho thing?" Hawk said.

"My expert does not know, which makes him very unhappy, but he says it's possible."

"So if someone found one," Sapp said.

"And kept their mouth shut," Hawk said.

"And perhaps purchased some land, cheap?"

I took my list out of my pocket and spread it on the table. Beside it I put the list of names of people who comprised the Saguaro Development Associates.

Everybody looked at both papers while I waited, watching enviously as Sapp polished off his sixth cup of coffee.

"Appears that we employed by Saguaro Associates," Hawk said.

"J. George Taylor," Bernard read aloud. "Luther M. Barnes, Henry F. Brown, Roscoe B. Land, Mary Louise Allard."

"Read it again, Bernard," Tedy Sapp said. "It was like listening to music."

Bernard ignored Sapp.

"Who's this Mary Louise Allard?" he said.

"Our own Mary Lou," I said. "Allard is her maiden name."

Everyone was quiet for awhile.

Then Vinnie said, "So what the hell does that mean?"

"Means we're in the middle of some kind of very big swindle," Sapp said.

"So whose side are we on?" Chollo said.

"I'm not sure," I said.

Hawk said, "Preacher might know."

"Yeah," I said. "He might."

chapter
52

Hawk and I sat in the dark on the front porch of The Jack Rabbit Inn drinking coffee and waiting for the light. When it finally arrived it came slowly, from behind us, seeping up over the hotel until it splashed gray, barely perceptible, onto the street in front of us. Hawk poured some more coffee from the Thermos. On the street there was no movement beyond the pale creeping illumination of the morning.

"You figure The Preacher an early riser?" Hawk said.

"I wanted everything in place."

"That's for sure."

We sat some more, sipping the coffee, looking at the inactive town, waiting. A yellow cat eased across the street and disappeared down the alley to the left of Mary Lou's storefront. Somewhere from the rooftops we could hear the twitter of birds.

"You know this ain't the best way," Hawk said.

I didn't say anything. The coffee smell was strong and comforting in the unsullied morning air.

"Best way," Hawk said, just as if I'd asked him, "be to pen them into that canyon and shoot them from up above."

I nodded.

"You know that, well as I do," Hawk said.

I nodded.

"But we going to do it this way."

I nodded.

"Being your faithful Afro-American companion ain't the easiest thing I ever done."

"But think of the positive side," I said.

"Which is?"

"Lemme get back to you on that," I said.

The light had spread across the street and past Mary Lou's storefront. Behind it came sunshine, still weak, but tinged with color, and carrying with it the promise of heat. I could feel the tension begin to knot. Hawk showed nothing. I'd never seen him show anything. He'd been cool for so long that if there were something to show, he probably wouldn't know it. Hawk drank more coffee, looking out over the rim of the cup along the now bright street.

"Need donuts," Hawk said.

"Try not to think about it," I said.

A few people began to appear. There were a couple of forty-ish women, in sneakers, shorts and tank tops power-walking on the sidewalk across the street. Some of the shops began to open. Doors were unlocked. Shades went up. Mary Lou, her hair held back by a blue-and-white polka dot headband, opened up on the other side. If she saw us she chose not to acknowledge it. In the hotel kitchen they were cooking bacon. The yellow cat reappeared, looking satisfied, and pattered down the sidewalk away from us, with his tail in the air.

"Bet he had a donut," Hawk said.

We were out of coffee. The street was bright now, and hot. Hawk seemed almost asleep in the chair beside me. His eyes were invisible behind his sunglasses, his gun concealed by a light silk warm-up jacket, the sleeves of which were tight over his upper arm.

Cars began to appear. More shops opened along the street. People spruced up for the morning walked past the hotel. Many of them trailed a hint of cologne and shampoo and shaving soap in the still air. One of Potshot's two police cruisers rolled slowly down toward the station.

Hawk watched it go by, his head turning slowly to follow it. Otherwise he was motionless.

"We follow that cruiser," he said, "we find donuts. Cops always know where they're donuts."

"Ever have a Krispy Kreme donut?" I said.

"No."

"Me either."

The sun had gotten high enough to shine straight into the windows of the shops across the street when they came. The old Scout was first, and even from a distance, as it turned into Main Street, I could see The Preacher, a contrast in pallor and black, sitting in front in the passenger seat. There were three other men, one of whom was almost certainly Pony, looming in the back seat, the Scout canted toward his side. Behind them came a ratty looking Jeep Wrangler that might once have been blue. There were four men in it.

"Maybe we can get a donut after," Hawk said.

He got up and took off his jacket. He was wearing his big .44 in a shoulder rig, and there was no further need to hide it. We walked across the street and stood in front of Mary Lou's store, Hawk on my left. The Preacher saw us and said something to the driver and he kept coming, and the second car followed, until he pulled up to a stop in front of us. The Preacher gestured and the two cars emptied, leaving only The Preacher and his driver still seated. Pony was in front of me. But he was aware of Hawk. I could see his eyes shift over and back. The others spread out around us in a semicircle. No one spoke. The Preacher seemed almost amused. Peripherally I could see Tedy Sapp's car move slowly in from the north end of the street, and Bobby Horse drive up from the south. Otherwise nothing moved in the street.

"So who are you," The Preacher said finally, "Wyatt fucking Earp?"

"I got some questions," I said.

The Preacher smiled.

"Pony," he said.

Pony took a step toward us and Hawk's gun barrel was suddenly pressed against his forehead. Guns came out all around us. The sound of hammers thumbed back was brisk in the hot silence. The Preacher showed no expression. Everything stopped stock-still. Behind The Preacher, to my left, Tedy Sapp was out of his car with his elbows resting on the hood and the shotgun leveled. To the right Bobby Horse was the same.

"The ball goes up," I said to Tedy Sapp, "kill The Preacher first."

My voice seemed blatant in the cavernous silence. The men in front of us glanced quickly around. Chollo walked out of the alley behind us, his Glock 9-millimeter handgun hanging loosely by his side.

"Let me kill him," Chollo said.

His voice was amplified by the silence as mine had been. Bernard J. Fortunato, with his shotgun at his shoulder, stepped out across the street. He didn't speak, but the shotgun was steady. From the second-floor window of the hotel I heard Vinnie. I couldn't see him, but the barrel of the Heckler & Koch was resting on the windowsill.

"No," Vinnie said. "Let me."

The silence seemed to twist and tighten. The frozen immobility of the scene seemed to squeeze in upon itself as though it would eventually shatter. I felt as if the pit of my stomach were clenched like a fist. Fortunately I was brave, clean and reverent, otherwise I might have been a little scared.

"You got any preference?" I said to The Preacher.

"This all the people you got?" The Preacher said.

"All we need at the moment," I said. "You know a guy named Morris Tannenbaum?"

The Preacher just stared at me.

"Morris tells me you and he had a deal," I said. "But he's mad at you now and wants you gone."

No one moved. The Preacher stared.

"Wants to pay us to get rid of you."

Hawk still pressed the muzzle of his .44 against Pony's forehead. I could hear Pony breathing.

"This guy Tannenbaum," The Preacher said. "He tell you this himself?"

"Ronny told us," I said.

The Preacher thought about that.

"So what's your question?" The Preacher said.

"What was your deal with Tannenbaum?"

The Preacher thought about that. I was pretty sure he wasn't brave, clean and reverent, but he didn't seem scared. In fact he didn't seem anything. His pale eyes showed nothing that I could detect. His voice was without inflection. His body language revealed nothing. In fact there was no body language. He sat motionless.

"Why should I tell you?" he said.

"Why not?" I said.

The Preacher looked slightly amused. His face like one of those close-up photographs of rattlesnakes where the snake seems almost mischievous.

"Why not," he said.

I waited, both of us ringed with weapons, both of us heated by the sun. Then The Preacher made some sort of facial gesture which was probably a smile.

"Why not," he said again. "Tannenbaum wanted us to run people out of Potshot."

"Why?"

"He never said."

"What did you get?"

"I got a fee. And we got whatever we could squeeze out of the town."

"Why is the deal off?"

"Maybe you should ask him."

"I don't have him in the middle of the street with six weapons pointed at him."

"You think I'm talking 'cause I'm scared?"

The Preacher's empty eyes held on me.

"No," I said.

He nodded slowly.

"We like what we got," The Preacher said. "We can live off this town forever, we don't use it up."

"So you didn't want to drive people out."

"Not till we got all there was."

"And Tannenbaum didn't like it."

"Fuck him," The Preacher said.

In the silence I could hear my own breathing. I felt stiff with tension. But I held still. Everyone was probably as tight as I was. I didn't want to start the shooting.

Carefully I said, "Who killed Steve Buckman?"

"Don't know."

"You got any connection with Mrs. Buckman?"

The Preacher made a cackling sound. It might have been a laugh.

"I'd like one," he said. "How about you, Pony? You like to make a connection with Mrs. Buckman?"

Pony was stock-still with the muzzle of Hawk's gun still against his forehead. It was a big gun, a .44 Magnum, with a stainless-steel finish, that made it glitter in the brutal sunshine. Neither of them had moved since the event began.

"Guess Pony ain't talking," The Preacher said.

"Thanks for your help," I said. "Time to go."

"Maybe we don't think so," The Preacher said.

"Maybe we don't care," I said.

The Preacher glanced slowly around at the circumstances. They were not to his advantage.

"Things start," The Preacher said. "We kill you first."

"We'll go together," I said.

The Preacher nodded, still assessing.

"We'll go," he said.

"Stay away from the town," I said.

The Preacher gave me another one of those amused rattlesnake stares. Then he nodded at the other men. And they got back in their vehicles. As they drove away, the muscles that had been so tight now became so loose I felt like I ought to lie down. Decompensating. The sound of the two vehicles faded. Sapp tossed his shotgun onto the back seat of his car and got in the driver's side. Bernard J. Fortunato got in with him. Chollo got in with Bobby Horse. Vinnie closed his hotel window and appeared a minute later with the rifle in a gun case. He got in with Chollo and Bobby Horse. The two cars pulled away. Hawk let the hammer back down on his big stainless-steel revolver and slid it back into its holster. He grinned at me.

"Cool," he said.

chapter
53

THE RATTLESNAKE CAFE served donuts. Hawk had four, and coffee. I wasn't hungry yet. I had coffee.

"You know he ain't going to let this go," Hawk said.

I nodded.

"Why he told you all that stuff. 'Cause he going to kill you."

"And you," I said.

"And everybody else," Hawk said. "So he don't care what he says to you."

"Which means he probably told the truth."

"Probably," Hawk said.

"Which means maybe Steve Buckman wasn't killed by the Dell."

Hawk broke a donut in half and took a significant bite.

"How 'bout the Saguaro Development Corporation?"

"Why would they kill him?"

"I just the hired hard case," Hawk said. "You the sleuth."

"They seem to be players," I said.

"Anybody in Saguaro Development got the balls to do it?"

"Mary Lou," I said.

Hawk nodded and finished his half donut. He took a sip of his coffee.

"Even though she cute and got a blond ponytail?"

"That usually eliminates a suspect," I said. "But somebody killed Buckman."

Dean Walker slipped into the booth next to me. He was looking clean and shiny. His uniform shirt was freshly pressed. He took his hat off and laid it crown down on the table in front of him.

"How're the donuts?" he said.

"No such thing as a bad donut," Hawk said.

He gestured at the waitress and she brought him coffee without further instruction.

"Did you have a little incident this morning?" Walker said to me.

"Big incident," I said.

"Pretty good," he said.

"You witness any of it?" I said.

Walker smiled.

"They're not going to let it go," he said.

"Probably not."

"There's seven of you," Walker said.

"You counted."

"There's about forty of them."

"Preacher says he didn't shoot Steve Buckman."

"Preacher ain't the most honest guy," Walker said.

"Nor the nicest," I said. "But what if he were telling the truth."

"Then it must have been somebody else," Walker said.

"That's why you're chief of police," I said.

"Nothing like a trained professional," Walker said. "What are you going to do about the Dell?"

"Wait and watch," I said.

"You ought to leave," he said.

I shrugged.

"You won't," Walker said. "Will you?"

I shook my head. Hawk was on his last donut. He seemed to be paying no attention. Which was, of course, a deception. Hawk paid attention to everything.

"Second best suggestion," Walker said. "Don't wait for them. Try to hit them first. I guarantee they're coming."

"Been urging that same course of action," Hawk said.

"You think Mary Lou might have killed her husband?"

"No."

"She might have," I said.

"No."

"Who's your candidate?" I said.

"If it wasn't the Dell?"

"Yeah."

"Might have been Ratliff."

"The producer?"

"Yeah. He followed her out here."

"Why?"

Walker didn't answer. He took a sip of his coffee, shook his head slightly and stirred more sugar into his cup.

"Unrequited love?" I said.

"He had an affair with her in L.A. It didn't mean anything. She and Steve were having a little trouble at the time."

"Last time I mentioned it," I said, "you said it was a lie."

"Did I say that?"

"You did."

"Probably before I learned the truth."

"Probably."

"He was annoying her," Walker said. "She complained to me and I had a talk with him."

"What'd he say?"

Walker continued to stir his coffee. The gesture was automatic, as if he'd forgotten about it.

"He admitted he followed her out here. Said he loved her. Said he just wanted to be near her."

"And you think he killed Buckman to clear the way for himself?"

"Might have. Might have heard that the Dell threatened Steve, and saw his chance. Shoot him and the Dell gets blamed."

"It's a theory," I said.

"Yep."

"Mary Lou's part of a group that's buying up real estate," I said.

"Good for her."

"Where's she get the money?"

"I look like H&R Block to you?"

"I'll take that to mean you don't know where she got the money."

"You take it to mean whatever the fuck you want to," Walker said.

"The mayor's part of the group," I said, "and J. George Taylor."

"Yeah?"

"Why do you suppose they're doing that?"

"Real estate's cheap around here."

"Because of the Dell?"

"Sure."

"So why does this group want it?"

"Maybe they have confidence in you," Walker said.

"Figure Potshot would boom without the Dell problem?"

Walker shook his head.

"Not enough water," he said. "We're at capacity."

"You ever sleep with Mary Lou?" I said.

"Hey," Walker said. "Who the fuck do you think you're talking to?"

"Do you know who Morris Tannenbaum is?"

"You think she slept with him?"

"Do you?"

"Watch your mouth pal. This is a lady you're talking about."

"Nothin' unladylike 'bout getting laid," Hawk said.

"Do you know Tannenbaum?" I said.

"No."

"But you're worried that Mary Lou might have slept with him?"

Walker stood up suddenly and picked up his hat and put it on.

"Fuck this," he said and left.

"Touchy," Hawk said.

"On this subject."

"You think he might be right 'bout Ratliff?"

"I think you're right about the question of ladies and sex."

"Good to be right about something," Hawk said. "You think she connected with Tannenbaum?"

"Everywhere I go in this thing I keep bumping into either her or him," I said.

"Don't mean they're connected," Hawk said.

"Ever since I signed on for this, I been trying to figure out where she's getting the money."

"Tannenbaum got some," Hawk said.

"He do," I said.

"You got any ideas how to find out about him?" Hawk said.

"I do," I said.

chapter
54

I SAT ON THE front porch with my Winchester rifle leaning against the porch railing beside me, and talked on the portable phone to Samuelson in L.A.

"You got any surveillance on Tannenbaum?" I said.

"Me? No."

"Organized Crime Unit, maybe?"

"Don't know. Lemme call you back."

I punched off, and sat and looked at the angular desert plants for awhile. Up the hill from the house, with a view of the road, Bobby Horse was taking his turn with one of the little black-and-yellow walkie-talkies we'd bought. In the house Chollo had the other one. As Bernard J. Fortunato had explained, being murdered in our beds would suck. Peripherally I saw movement in the brush at the right corner of the house. I put down the cell phone and picked up the Winchester. A deer came delicately out from the cover, stopped short, and stared at me with its enormous dark eyes. I put the gun back down. The deer twitched its over-sized ears a couple of times. I didn't move. After more staring and twitching, the deer ate a leaf off of one of the dry desert plants, then did a big leap into the woods and vanished.

The portable phone rang. It was Samuelson.

"OCU's got nothing going on with Tannenbaum," he said. "But the Feds do."

"FBI?"

"Yep."

"And?"

"And they are not sharing it with us."

"Nice cooperation," I said. "You got anybody who'll whisper it to you?"

"Maybe, but then I got to whisper stuff to him."

"Okay," I said. "I know a guy."

"I was sure you would," Samuelson said, and broke the con-nection.

I went in the house and looked up a number in my address book and came back out and sat and dialed it up. A man answered on the first ring.

"Yes?"

I said, "Ives?"

"Who's calling?"

"Spenser."

There was a pause while Ives processed me through his mem-ory banks.

"Well," he said. "Lochinvar."

"I need a favor," I said.

"In which case you will then owe me one."

"There's a guy named Morris Tannenbaum. Runs most of the rackets east of L.A."

"Really?" Ives said.

"The Bureau has surveillance on him," I said. "I need to talk with someone who has access to it."

"Our cousins at the Bureau are not usually forthcoming with surveillance data," Ives said.

"Gimme a guy to talk with," I said.

I waited.

"Wilbur," he said. "Wilbur Harris."

I waited.

"I'll call Wilbur, give him a heads up on your behalf."

"Got the phone number?"

He gave it to me.

"Call Wilbur in half an hour," Ives said, and broke the connection.

Bernard J. Fortunato came onto the porch carrying a street sweeper.

"Lot of firepower for a guy your size," I said.

"Fifty rounds of twelve-gauge shotgun shells," Bernard said. "Automatic. Vinnie showed me how to modify it."

"He show you how to hit what you shoot at?" I said.

"Already knew that," Bernard said.

"I guess that thing makes accuracy less of an issue."

"You think I'm not accurate?" Bernard said. "I'm accurate."

"I hope so," I said. "I don't want you shooting one of us with that thing."

I was watching the brush where the deer had silently moved.

There was always some sort of muffled visceral tug when I looked at a wild animal. I never really knew what the tug was. But I liked it when it happened.

"You sure they're going to come?" Bernard said.

"They'll come."

"We backed them down pretty good in town," Bernard said.

"There's forty of them and seven of us," I said. "You think The Preacher doesn't know that?"

"So?"

"So why fight us when the odds are even?"

"Then why don't we try what Bobby Horse says? Lock them up in the valley and shoot them from up above?"

I shook my head.

"Lot of us think it's the way to go," Bernard said.

"I don't," I said.

"Maybe we should vote."

"Maybe I should make my phone call," I said.

Bernard shrugged and walked down to the other end of the porch. I called Wilbur Harris.

"I don't usually do this," Harris said. "But our mutual friend is entitled to a favor."

"You got surveillance on a guy in L.A. named Morris Tannenbaum?"

"No further mention of names, please," Harris said. "We have him under consideration."

"Phone tap?" I said.

"Yes."

"Visual surveillance?"

"Yes."

"Got a bug in the house?"

"Yes. In his study."

"How long?"

"Two years."

"He make you?"

"I think he's spotted the visual. They all assume they're tapped. I don't think he's wise to the bug."

"Can you give me the logs from the bug?"

"Sure," Harris said. "Maybe do your tax returns for you?"

"And transcripts?"

"You can't have the transcripts. It would take too long to copy them."

"How about I give you a few names and if you come across them, you send me their transcripts?"

"Gimme the names. I'll see what we can do."

I gave him some names.

"If they're all in the logs it's too many," he said. "We got a serious problem staffing clerical help."

"God forbid you do the Xeroxing yourself."

"God forbid."

"Can you overnight them to me?"

"And what do we get?" Harris said.

"I think Tannenbaum's tied to a big swindle," I said. "If I can bust my end of it, you might get Tannenbaum."

"Gimme your address."

I did.

chapter
55

VINNIE WAS UP on the hill with his walkie-talkie. The rest of us were on the porch. I sat on the railing. Hawk leaned on the post by the porch steps. Tedy Sapp was making drinks.

"We have a position," Chollo said, "for your consideration, jefe."

"We?"

"All us, for whom I, a simple Latino, am honored to speak."

"That the same as simpleton?" I said.

"I do not think so. We are thinking that it makes no sense for us to sit here and wait for the Dell to attack us, when we could go out and slyly shoot them while they were still in their hole."

"If we were to be successful, we'd have to massacre pretty much all of them," I said.

"Sí."

"I don't want to do that," I said.

"On the other hand, señor, we do not wish them to massacre us."

"I was thinking maybe there'd be a third option," I said. "Maybe I can bust this murder case and then maybe we won't have to fight the Dell."

"We would run?"

"It's a third option," I said.

Nobody else said anything. Chollo took the drink that Tedy Sapp handed him, and took a sip and held it happily in his mouth for a moment before he swallowed it.

"You were not so reticent about shooting in Proctor when we were after that cop's wife," Chollo said.

"We weren't shooting fish in a barrel."

"We were risking women and children."

"They were risking the women and children," I said. "We were getting Belson's wife out of there, and it was worth a massacre if it came to that."

"And this situation is not worth a massacre?"

"No."

Chollo thought about that. Everyone else was quiet.

"You do not have to do it," Chollo said, without anger. "We can do it, and when we have you can solve your murder."

Sapp handed me some beer in a long-neck bottle. Blue Moon, a personal favorite. I had a pull.

"No," I said.

Chollo didn't seem offended. Thoughtfully he rocked back in his chair. Bobby Horse sat beside him, both feet flat of the floor. Bernard was in another rocker, the second walkie-talkie on the table beside him. Tedy Sapp had stopped tending bar and was leaning on the wall, his arms folded. Even in repose, Sapp looked as if he were flexing. Chollo balanced his chair by touching his feet to the floor just often enough to keep the chair steady. He looked at Hawk.

"I'm with him," Hawk said and nodded toward me.

"You would have a problem with shooting them?" Chollo said.

"No."

"But you won't?"

"No."

Chollo nodded slowly. He looked at Bobby Horse.

"We could go back to L.A.," Bobby Horse said.

"Sí."

Chollo looked at Sapp.

"I vote for the massacre," Sapp said.

"Bernard?" Chollo said.

"I just as soon shoot all of them that we can," Bernard said.

Chollo turned back toward me.

"But I got something else," Bernard said.

Chollo waited. Loose in his chair. Peaceful.

"We ought to do what he says."

"Because?" Chollo asked.

"Because we said we would."

"And we cannot change our mind?"

"Bernard J. Fortunato's word is good," he said.

All of us were quiet, staring at Bernard. Finally Tedy Sapp spoke.

"You're so fucking little," he said. "I didn't know you had a word."

"You got to keep your word more," Bernard said, "if you're small."

Chollo was looking past me, toward the road.

"Hello FedEx," he said.

A Federal Express truck pulled up in front of the house and the driver got out with an envelope.

"Mr. Spenser?" he said.

"Me," I said.

He handed me the letter. I signed his little Etch A Sketch, and he went to his truck and drove away. I opened the envelope. Inside was a thick sheaf of computer printout. I slipped it back in the envelope and looked around the porch.

"You guys come to any conclusions?" I said.

"Bobby Horse and I will stay," Chollo said.

"Me too," Tedy Sapp said.

"Vinnie tole me he'd do what I did," Hawk said.

I looked around the porch. With the possible exception of Sapp, these were bad men who had done bad things.

"Okay," I said.

No one had anything else to say.

"Whyn't you read that list?" Hawk said.

chapter
56

I READ THE TRANSCRIPTS first. There were three: one George, who seemed to be a drug dealer, one Henry, who sounded like a bookie, and one Lou (female) talking about water resources in a place called Potshot (no state mentioned). The entry was dated a month before she hired me. Some of it was the kind of trivial chatter that people have before they settle in. Then I came to it.

TANNENBAUM: Fix us a couple more drinks, will you baby?

LOU: I'd love to.

TANNENBAUM: Oh man, that hits the spot.

LOU: To you, Morrie.

TANNENBAUM: Preacher's fucking us. I think he knows about the water.

LOU: Steve told him.

TANNENBAUM: That fucking blow. He's like a loose fucking can

...on. Bragging about being a bad guy. He's going to fuck up this fucking deal if we don't do something about him. I told you we needed to do something about him.

LOU: *I can fix it.*

TANNENBAUM: *How you going to fix it?*

LOU: *I know a person who will do it.*

TANNENBAUM: *I don't want you hiring nobody. Lotta deals go south 'cause some fucking hired guy can't keep his fucking mouth shut.*

LOU: *Person I'm thinking of will be fine. He'll do anything I say.*

TANNENBAUM: *You fucking him?*

LOU: *Just enough.*

TANNENBAUM: *To keep him under control?*

LOU: *Un-huh.*

TANNENBAUM: *That what you doing to me?*

LOU: *Nobody can keep you under control, Morrie.*

(Sound of sexual activity.)

TANNENBAUM: *Come on you little bitch. You know you want it.*

LOU: *Morrie, I'm not going to fuck you right here on the floor.*

TANNENBAUM: *You'd fuck me in the middle of the I-5 freeway if you needed to.*

LOU: *Come on Morrie. Let's go to bed.*

It was pretty clear that they were talking about Steve Buckman's impending murder, though no one quite said it. And the feds were willing to let some guy named Steve get "fixed" rather than reveal their bug on Tannenbaum. I knew they'd say, "If we can put Tannenbaum out of business, we'll save a lot more lives than maybe this guy Steve who may get killed." And I knew they were probably right. The most good for the most people and all that. I was glad I didn't have to think that way.

I thought about Lou with Morris Tannenbaum and felt crawly.

Then I found myself smiling, alone, in the badly furnished living room of a rented house in a remote town. I had a genuine clue implicating my client in her husband's murder and my first reaction was disappointment in her sex life.

Then I wondered who the someone was that would do anything she told him. I knew of two guys in Potshot that she might control—Mark Ratliff and Dean Walker. Given what I was learning about Mary Lou, there might have been twenty others. Anyone who would bop Morris Tannenbaum . . . and I kind of liked Walker. I hoped it wasn't him.

I went through the logs looking for familiar names. There were none. If anyone else from Potshot was talking to Morris Tannenbaum, it wasn't someone I knew.

chapter
57

VICKI WAS DOING turquoise today. Turquoise sundress, and a turquoise headband restraining her dark hair. Her long fingernails were turquoise, and she wore a heavy turquoise and silver necklace with matching earrings.

"Mr. Ratliff isn't in," she said after she'd admired the way I walked to her reception desk.

"When do you expect him?"

"I don't know," she said. "He's . . . he hasn't been in all week."

"Have you talked with him?"

"I called his home. I was worried. All I got was his machine."

"On which you left a message?"

"Several," she said.

"And no call back?"

"No."

"You report him missing?"

"I called Chief Walker," she said. "He said that he was sure nothing untoward had happened."

"Untoward?"

"That's the word he used," Vicki said.

"I love a good vocabulary," I said. "Don't you?"

"Of course."

Walker's words must have comforted Vicki. She didn't seem consumed with worry. She was still looking at me like an appraiser. I wondered if the look were lustful. I sucked in my stomach.

"Give me his home address," I said. "I'll go check on him."

"I don't know if I should," Vicki said.

"Of course you should."

"You are a detective," she said.

"You bet I am."

She appraised me some more. It seemed a cool appraisal, but it might have masked lust. I smiled reassuringly. Big smile. Wide. Friendly. Honest. You can count on me. She smiled back, and wrote Ratliff's home address on the back of a business card and handed me the card. I must use that smile only for good.

Mark Ratliff's house was small and stuccoed and faux Spanish, with red tile on the roof. A BMW sports car was parked under a carport to the right of the house. Several days worth of *The Los Angeles Times* were scattered near the front door. I looked at them. The earliest was last Tuesday; the most recent was this morning. I rang the bell. No one answered. I walked around the house. There was a small patio out back and a sliding door that opened onto it. The locks on sliding doors often worked badly. I tried the door. It didn't open. I looked inside. The door was held in place by a short stick that prevented it from sliding. Sticks worked well. I walked around the house again. No alarm signs. No *protected by* stickers in the windows. I went back to the patio, took my gun out and broke the glass in the sliding door enough so I could reach in and remove the stick. Then I slid the door open and went in. It was cool. The air-conditioning made a quiet sound. Everything else was still. The house was empty. I would look carefully, but you almost always know when a house is empty as soon as you walk in.

The house was orderly but not anal. Beside a Barcalounger in the living room was a copy of *The Los Angeles Times*, dated last Monday. It was scattered on the floor, the way it would be if someone had been reading it. On the floor next to the right side of the Barcalounger, among the newspaper pages, was a squat glass with a half-inch of water in it. I picked it up and sniffed. Scotch maybe. The ice had melted.

I walked through the house. All seemed to be in order. In Ratliff's bedroom were three pieces of matched luggage of descending sizes. Lined up side by side, they just fit the width in the back of his closet. In the linen closet was a tan pigskin shaving kit. It was empty. There were sunglasses, some keys, and loose change on top of the bureau in his bedroom. There was a toothbrush in the slot in his bathroom. An electric shaver sat in its recharging base on a glass shelf under the mirror.

In the kitchen there was milk in the stainless steel refrigerator. I smelled it. Spoiled. The refrigerator reminded me of Susan's. There wasn't much in there. Producers are probably too important to cook, unlike Susan, who was too impatient.

Ratliff had converted what was probably once a dining room into a den. There was an imposing desk in front of the back window. I looked through it, and found nothing much beyond some bills, a couple dozen Bic pens, and a roll of Tums. I punched up his answering machine. There were two calls from Vicki, and no others. I picked up his phone. Dial tone. I browsed his computer. There was an online banking folder, a stationery folder, and a screenplay folder. I opened it. There was a 135-page screenplay titled *The Millennium Beast*. The title page said it was by Mark Ratliff. The format was very professional. I read a couple of pages. It was horrendous. Ratliff probably had a hit on his hands.

It took me another couple of hours to go through everything in the house. When I finished I went back into his living room and sat on the couch. All I knew for sure was that Ratliff wasn't there. His luggage seemed intact. He hadn't taken his shaving kit. His toothbrush was still in the bathroom, and so was his electric razor. He might have had another piece of luggage. He might have another home fully stocked with razors and toothbrushes. But his car was still in the carport. His keys were still on his bureau.

Ratliff appeared to have left without taking anything, by means unknown, for reasons unknown. At least, unknown to me.

chapter
58

I<small>T WAS JUST</small> after sunrise. We were at breakfast. Like our ancestors. No television. No night life. We went to bed early and got up early. Bernard had cooked up hash and eggs. Sapp was already on his third coffee.

"When you think the Dell will come?" Sapp said.

He didn't sound apprehensive. He seemed simply curious.

"They come before we're through solving his murder," Hawk said, "we got something to think about. There about forty of them and about seven of us."

"Which is about six to one," I said.

"I'da never figured that out," Hawk said.

"Is it a genetic thing?" I said.

"Yeah. We good at tap dancing, though."

"I figure we need to find a way to make it more even," I said.

"Try to force them to split up?"

"Something like that. So we can end up, say, seven on six, our favor."

"I been thinking the same thing," Chollo said. " 'Cept for the numbers. We no good at numbers either."

"So what are you good at?" I said.

"Playing the guitar, singing sad songs."

"Just what we need."

"Sí."

"That's what cavalry is for," Sapp said.

"Cavalry," Bernard said from the stove. "I can't ride no fucking horse."

"Get you a pony," Sapp said.

He looked at me.

"You get what I mean?"

"Yes," I said. "Bring a lot of force to bear on a small section of the enemy by moving a small force around rapidly."

Sapp shot me with his forefinger and thumb. He nodded several times.

"Mobility," he said.

"That what you meant whyn't you say so?" Bernard said. "Stead of that pony shit."

"Who we got for cavalry?" Vinnie said.

"Us," Chollo said.

"So," Hawk said, "we don't figure out what to do with them. We figure out what to do with us."

I put some more ketchup on the hash. You can't have too much ketchup on hash. I ate some and had a bite of toast and a swallow of coffee. Balance is important. I didn't say anything. One of the things I'd learned from Susan was the creative use of silence.

"How about you, Kemo Sabe?" Chollo said to Bobby Horse. "You got any Kiowa battle secrets?"

"Get them to circle the wagons," Bobby Horse said. "And ride around and around them."

"I got firing points laid out," Vinnie said. "So the field of fire covers all the approaches to the house."

"But we stay in the house we still back to six on one," Hawk said.

Vinnie nodded. My breakfast wasn't coming out even. I took another piece of toast from the platter Bernard had put on the table.

"So we need to get out of the house," Chollo said.

"We probably in better shape than they are," Hawk said. "We get higher than them, they going to be laboring they have to chase us uphill."

"Especially," I said, "if they have to chase us a lot."

chapter
59

I WAS ALONE ON the front porch when Dean Walker pulled his cruiser up in front of the house. Hatless, he got out and came up the front walk, his eyes masked behind his aviator shades.

"Holding the fort?" he said.

"Valiantly," I said.

"You still got troops?"

"Yep."

"Handy?"

"Yep."

"Good," Walker said. "You'll need them."

"Because?"

"Because today's the day," Walker said.

"For?"

"For the Dell to come down on you."

"How many?"

"All of them."

"When?"

Walker smiled.

"Can't say for sure," he said. "But they aren't early risers."

"But you know it's today."

"Yeah."

"How would you know that?" I said.

"I'm the police," Walker said.

"And where do you stand?" I said.

"Out of the way," Walker said.

"So why'd you warn me?"

"Civic duty," Walker said.

I nodded. We looked at each other for a moment. Then Walker turned and walked back to his car and got in and drove off. I watched him go. Then I picked up my Winchester and walked up the hill behind the house. The desert was empty, sprawled in harsh metallic silence under the oppressive sun.

Bobby Horse was on lookout with binoculars around his neck and his BAR leaning in the shade of a rock.

"Where's Hawk?" I said.

"Down near the road. They're running things through."

I said, "The Dell's on its way."

Bobby Horse scanned the landscape with his binoculars.

"Don't see them," he said.

I picked up the walkie-talkie from the shade beside the BAR.

"Hawk," I said.

He answered.

"Bring everyone back up to the lookout," I said. "Dell's coming."

" 'Bout time," Hawk said.

"After Bobby Horse spots them with the glasses," I said when we were gathered, "it'll take them about fifteen minutes to arrive."

"What if they come another way?" Bernard said.

"There isn't another way," I said, "except over the mountain behind us. They're not that industrious."

Hawk nodded.

"We put Vinnie on the right, Chollo in the center, and Bernard Whosis on the left."

"Fortunato," Bernard said. "Goddamn it, Bernard J. Fortunato."

"Right," Hawk said. "You on the left. Me and Sapp and Bobby Horse start in the center, behind Chollo, and bust our ass left or right, depending on what's going down."

"Like in *Zulu*," Sapp said.

"Tha's where I learned all my military tactics," Hawk said. "Spenser?"

"I'll freelance," I said.

"I sort of guessed that," Hawk said. "We already have water and ammunition stashed at each firing position."

He had forgotten his jive accent again.

"Drink a lot of water," I said.

"That way," Chollo said, "we run out of ammunition we can piss on them."

"What you gonna do freelancing?" Vinnie said.

"I thought I'd hide under the bed until you guys won," I said.

"We'll let you know," Vinnie said.

"But in case I'm not under the bed," I said. "I'll be down below the house, behind them if they come in."

"And?" Sapp said.

"And I want to be the first one to shoot."

"If possible," Hawk said.

"If possible."

I turned and started down the hill. After ten steps I turned and said to Hawk, "Good hunting." To my ear I sounded amazingly like Stewart Granger.

Hawk grinned and gave me a thumbs-up.

"Gringos watch too many movies," Chollo said.

"African Americans, too," Hawk said.

"Sí."

I went on down the hill.

chapter
60

THEY CAME IN a long, relentless line of trucks and motor-cycles. As they moved past me onto the dirt road to the house, dust lingered behind them, kicked up by their passage.

Mongol hordes.

I lay behind my rock in a clump of cactus as they passed, with the sun pressing down on my back and the Winchester laid across the rock. I had a bag of ammunition and some water. I wore a Browning 9mm, on my right hip, and the Smith & Wesson .38 butt forward on my left side. The line pulled up in front of the house and spread into a wide semicircle, the motors still running. The thick smell of exhaust fouled the intense desert air. They were so used to intimidating people, and they had arrived in such numbers, that they were arrogant, and arrogance made them stupid. They put out no scouts, and paid no attention to the possibility of ambush. Their only concession to the possibility that we

might put up a fight was to dismount their vehicles and stay behind them, except The Preacher. He sat upright and almost regal
in the passenger seat beside the Mexican driver, while Pony
threw a leg over the side, and climbed out of the back seat of the
Scout, and waddled fearsomely to the front door, carrying an assault rifle. The collective motors grumbled in the silence.

"Spenser," Pony said loudly.

Nothing.

"Preacher's here," Pony said.

Nothing.

The Preacher gestured and nine men moved out from behind
the vehicles and clustered behind Pony. All of them had long
guns.

"You come out or we come in," Pony blared.

We didn't come out. Pony jacked a shell up into the chamber
of the assault rifle, kicked open the door and went in. The other
nine guys crowded in behind them, bumping into each other and
jamming up in the door before they got through. It didn't appear that they'd given this a lot of planning. In three or four minutes they came back out, this time taking turns through the door.

"Looks like they run," Pony said.

The Preacher began to look up the hill

"They didn't run far," he said. "Spread out. Look for them."

I levered a round into the chamber of the Winchester. The
Mexican driver heard the sound and jumped from the Scout with
a long-barreled revolver in his hand, in a half crouch, looking
toward my rock. I eased the rifle over the rock, aiming so that
the Mexican driver was sitting on my front sight. He saw the
movement, and snapped off a shot that spanged off the rock. I
shot him in the middle of the chest and he fell straight backward

and lay on the ground beside the Scout. The remainder of the Dell surged toward my rock, and my colleagues opened up from the hillside. The Preacher sat bolt upright in the Scout.

"Pony," he said, "take five men and clean up behind the rock. The rest of you spread out up the hill. Don't bunch up."

With my ammo and my water I moved down from behind my rock, and crossed the road behind them and took new shelter in a small wash behind the house.

The gunfire from the hill badly damaged the center of the Dell advance. Stalled, the survivors pinned down behind whatever cover they could find. I could hear the fast boom boom of Bernard's street sweeper. Then the firing stopped. The silence was startling. From the wash I could see Pony and his team moving carefully up behind the rock where I had been. From the hillside the gunfire erupted again, and the right flank of the Dell line washed back and hunkered down. But the left flank surged forward as if responding to the ebbing of the right, and now their gunfire was on the top of the hill. From behind my former rock I heard Pony yell to The Preacher.

"He's not here."

"Then get your asses up the hill," The Preacher said.

The gunfire was dense, and almost entirely from the left. My guys must have clustered up on that flank. The Dell line in the center began to move again, and the right side surged back as if having reached low tide. It was making its natural rebound. There were too many of them. We were in danger of getting overrun.

I squirmed along the wash and scuttled, bent nearly double, up the hillside on the right. Twenty yards behind the advancing Dell troops, I took up residence behind another rock and began to snipe the advance. I knocked two of them down before they

realized where I was shooting from. I saw four of them peel off
and head cautiously back down the hillside, looking for me. I had
a map of the area in my head. I'd walked it days ago. I knew where
every rock was, every depression in the ground, every growth of
arid vegetation sufficient to hide behind. I picked off one of the
people looking for me, and dove and rolled into a little gully with
a fringe of brush along the lip. Gunfire scattered around the rock.
The smell of it hung heavy in the stifling air. My eardrums hurt.
From the other side of the line, behind the advancing left flank
of the Dell forces, I heard the crack of a rifle, close enough to
me to be sharp against the general din of arms. Somebody had
gotten behind the Dell lines on the left and was picking them off
from behind as I was on the right. It was as if everything were
balanced precisely until the second sniper showed up. He was too
much. The balance teetered. The Dell assault held for a moment,
hanging on to the top of the hill, and then broke. These were
not professionals. It started as a hesitation, then a halt, then a withdrawal, and, as the withdrawal moved back down the hill it picked
up speed, and turned very quickly into a running away. Two guys
ran right past me as I lay in my gully. They were intent on leaving. They paid no attention to me. I didn't shoot them. I stood
and ran through the rout, weaving among the running men like
a kick returner. I was looking for The Preacher.

I found him standing stiffly upright beside the Jeep, as his
troops flowed past him. He was making no attempt to stop the
route. He seemed frozen by it. I stopped beside him holding the
Winchester muzzle-down but cocked.

"Now you know how Custer felt," I said.

The Preacher turned his head and stared at me. He didn't say
anything. The retreat tumbled past us and then it was gone. My

ears rang from the firing. The smell of the gunfire was everywhere. My shirt was soaked with sweat and clung to my back. I
could hear my breath heaving in and out. Up the hill there was
movement. My side. The first person I saw was Tedy Sapp. He
was shirtless, carrying Bernard J. Fortunato in his arms, as if
Bernard weighed no more than a puppy. Bernard's right pant leg
was wet with blood and a piece of a shirt, presumably Tedy
Sapp's, was tied around his thigh. Hawk was behind him, one arm
around Bobby Horse, who leaned on him heavily as they edged
down. Vinnie came behind them with Chollo. Chollo was bleed-
ing on one side of his neck.

"They shot me," Bernard said, as they came up to where I
stood. "Fuckers shot me right in the goddamned leg. In the fucking leg. Hurts like a bastard."

"Great shooter," Sapp said. "Hit a target as small as you."

"Bobby?" I said.

"Tore up my left knee," he said.

Chollo stood in front of The Preacher for a moment and then
grinned at him.

He said, "We deal in lead, friend."

The Preacher showed no sign that he'd heard Chollo, or that
he knew we were there. He was still rigid beside the ratty Scout.
Tedy Sapp put Bernard down in the shade of the Scout and let
him lean on the front right tire. Hawk helped Bobby Horse onto
the ground beside him. Bobby didn't lean. He lay flat on his back
and stared straight into the pain. I looked at my watch. The
whole fight had taken twenty minutes.

"What about your neck?" Vinnie said.

"A piece of rock," Chollo said, "chipped off and nicked me."

There was movement on the left periphery. Five of us turned

to shoot, and Dean Walker came out of the scrub, where not so long ago the deer had walked, carrying an AR-15, and looking a little sweaty. His radio was strapped to his belt, the microphone clipped to one of his shoulder epaulets.

"I already called for some EMTs," he said.

He spoke to The Preacher.

"You're under arrest," he said, "for assault with deadly force, for trespassing, and probably for leading an insurrection. You have the right to remain silent. You have the right to an attorney. . . ."

From out of sight, faintly at first, down the road toward town, I could hear the whoop of the ambulance siren growing louder.

chapter 61

Showered and shaved, comforted by ten hours sleep behind me and six buckwheat cakes, I sat in Dean Walker's office drinking coffee from a white mug that said *Santa Monica* on it in red script. He drank from one just like it.

"Been a cop too long," Walker said. "I couldn't let it slide."

"Good," I said. "How about the Dell."

"Most of them have split," Walker said. "I managed to convince the county that the ones left were squatting on county land, and there's a bunch of sheriff's deputies up there now evicting them."

"Also good," I said. "How about your cops?"

"They resigned," Walker said.

"Didn't care to fight the Dell?"

"Not at these prices," Walker said.

My coffee was gone. I went over to the Mr. Coffee on the top of the file and poured another cup. I brought it back and sat down again across from Walker.

"I wish I owned a swell cup like this," I said.

"I know," Walker said. "I feel very lucky."

"Preacher got anything to say?"

"Not yet."

"He will," I said, "when it's time to save his ass."

Walker smiled.

"How cynical," he said.

"I'm trying to change," I said.

"Never too late," he said. "Cawley Dark's coming down to talk to The Preacher about Steve Buckman."

"I don't think The Preacher did it," I said.

"He did something," Walker said.

"I don't want to bag him for something he didn't do," I said.

"I'll take what I can get," Walker said.

We were quiet. We drank some coffee in the cool empty room. Mr. Coffee had done a nice job. The coffee was good.

"What about Mark Ratliff?" I said.

"I don't got Mark Ratliff in a cell," Walker said. "I got The Preacher."

"And you're willing to railroad him?"

"The Preacher's a creep," Walker said. "He was out to kill you. He's probably killed a lot of people. Just because maybe he didn't kill Stevie Buckman is no reason not to hang him for it."

"How cynical," I said.

"I'm trying to change," Walker said, and smiled.

We drank some more coffee. The hushed sound of the air-conditioning made the room seem even quieter than it would have with no sound at all.

"Ratliff's missing," I said.

"That's what his secretary says."

"You been looking for him?"

"I'm a one-man department," Walker said. "I been kinda busy."

"I owe you for that time in the street," I said. "And I owe you more for showing up when you did yesterday."

Walker nodded and said nothing.

"But I don't owe you everything there is."

"You don't owe me nothing," Walker said. "I was doing what I'm supposed to do."

"And now you're not. I came out here to find out who killed Steve Buckman, not just clear the case."

Walker was silent.

Then he said, "I think maybe it's time you went home."

"Not yet," I said.

"Whatever you might think," Walker said, "I'm what this place has got for law. I could shoot you dead for resisting arrest, and no one would say shit."

"Someone might," I said.

Walker smiled again, but not because he was happy.

"You're an optimistic bastard," he said.

I finished my coffee and put the empty mug down on the edge of Walker's desk and stood up.

"Persistent, too," I said.

chapter
62

IT WAS OUR last breakfast together. We were eating omelets with onions, made, and beautifully, by me. Everyone was at the table in the kitchen, except Bobby Horse, who was propped up on a couch that Chollo and Hawk had dragged in from the living room. A local doctor had done what he could for Bobby Horse, put a cast on the knee, and had given him a large supply of Percocet. The Percocet made him quieter, which I would have thought impossible.

Bernard J. Fortunato wasn't as badly hurt. The bullet had gone through his thigh without breaking any bone. It had destroyed some of the tissue around the entry hole, and it would take awhile to heal. Bernard had Percocet too, and its effect was to make him more talkative. Between him and Bobby Horse, they averaged out about normal.

"So what I wanna know," Bernard said, sitting sideways at the table with his injured leg sticking out toward the stove, "didn't we ambush those Dell guys and shoot them up pretty good?"

"We did," I said.

I put an omelet on a plate with some biscuits. Chollo took it to Bobby Horse.

"You need me to feed you?" Chollo said.

Bobby Horse shook his head.

"So if we was going to ambush the fuckers anyway," Bernard said. "How come we didn't do it first, climb up there and shoot them down right in the canyon?"

"They hadn't come for us then," I said.

"That's why I got fucking shot," Bernard said.

I nodded. I was at the stove again, making another omelet. You have to make omelets in small batches or they don't work. And the pan needs to be cured, and the heat needs to be right. You don't just break a bunch of eggs.

"I don't get it," Bernard said.

"You get used to it," Vinnie said.

"But we did the same fucking thing," Bernard said. "And I got fucking shot doing it, and so did Bobby Horse."

The current omelet had firmed up just enough. I folded it over, shook it around in the pan a minute, and slid it onto a plate. I gave it to Bernard.

"Are you going to explain it?" Bernard said to me.

"Just eggs and some pan-fried onions," I said.

"I'm not talking about the fucking omelet, for crissake," Bernard said. "Vinnie, you know what I'm talking about."

Vinnie shrugged.

"You get it?" Bernard said to Vinnie.

"Yeah."

"And?"

"You get used to it," Vinnie said.

"Well it's fucking crazy," Bernard said.

Hawk put his coffee cup down and rested his forearms on the table.

"No," he said. "It's not crazy."

Bernard looked a little scared. Most people were afraid of Hawk, but there was heft in Hawk's voice that Bernard had never heard before. A lot of people hadn't.

"It's what makes him different than you," Hawk said, "or me or Vinnie, or Chollo or Bobby Horse."

"What about Tedy?" Bernard said.

Bernard had the attention span of a hummingbird.

"Don't know about Tedy," Hawk said. "Might be more like Spenser."

"Except for the queer part," Sapp said.

" 'Cept that," Hawk said. "The rest of us, we see something that needs to be done, we do it. We don't much care how we do it. Spenser thinks that how you do it is as important as what you do."

I realized what had startled Bernard. There was no mockery in Hawk's voice. None of his usual up-alley, self-amused, ghetto bebop. Bernard stared at him. They all did, except me. I was working on a new omelet.

"Why?" Bernard said.

Hawk grinned suddenly.

"So he be different than us."

I don't think Bernard got it. But everyone else seemed to, and

Bernard, Percocet-addled though he was, sensed it and shut up. The rest of breakfast conversation was devoted to women we had known.

After breakfast I sat on the front porch with Hawk and drank more coffee.

"I don't need to sleep at night, anyway," I said.

Chollo came out helping Bobby Horse. He got him arranged in the back seat of the car, with one leg out straight, and came back up the steps.

"You got everything?" I said.

"Guns are in the trunk, jefe."

"What about Bobby Horse?" I said.

"Mr. del Rio has a friend at UCLA Medical Center," Chollo said.

"I didn't know del Rio had friends."

"When he needs them," Chollo said. "Like you."

I put out my right hand, clenched in a fist. Chollo tapped his fist lightly on top of it, nodded at Hawk and walked to the car. Bobby Horse never glanced back as they drove away.

"We through here?" Hawk said.

"Everybody but me," I said.

Vinnie came out with Tedy Sapp. Bernard J. Fortunato hobbled along with them, Tedy had an arm around him holding him up. Bernard had one arm around Sapp's shoulder.

"We're going to Vegas," Bernard said. "I'm going to drink six Mai Tais and fuck six women the first day."

"Better do it the other way around," I said.

"I'll take the rental," Sapp said. "Drop Bernard off. Turn it in at the airport. Fly home from Vegas."

"My best to the opthalmologist," I said.

Sapp grinned.

"And to the shrink," Sapp said.

The three of them headed for the car and got Bernard in the back. Sapp got in the driver's side. Vinnie went around to the passenger side. He stopped before he got in and looked over the roof of the car.

"I left my guns all packed," Vinnie said. "Drive them home for me."

"You're going to Vegas?" I said.

"One drive between Boston and here is enough," Vinnie said. "Gonna help Bernard with the Mai Tais and the broads, then I'll fly home."

"Viva Las Vegas," I said.

"You gonna pay me?"

"When I get back to Boston."

Vinnie nodded.

"I packed my guns in the back of the Explorer," he said. "I'll pick them up in Boston."

"Spenser's long haul," I said. "No package too illegal."

Vinnie nodded at Hawk and at me, and slid into the car, and the car slid into gear and went down the road. "You still worrying 'bout the guy got killed?"

"Steve Buckman."

"Going to stick around until you sort that out?" Hawk said.

"Yes."

Hawk had his feet up on the railing, his hands locked behind his head and his chair tilted back. He looked out at the sage and cactus and shale and sand that stretched in front of the house up the hill.

"Me too," he said.

chapter
63

"ARE YOU OKAY?" Susan said when I called her.

"I'm fine," I said. "Just wanted to listen to your voice for a little while."

"It'll have to be a very little while. I have another patient in . . . three minutes."

"Maybe he'll be late," I said.

"He's never late. When are you coming home?"

"Not quite yet. I got everything done but one thing."

"Have you done your thing with the Dell yet?"

"Yep."

"Successful?"

"Yep."

"I was scared about that," Susan said.

"Me too."

"What's the one thing?"

"Who killed Steve Buckman?"

"Will it take long?"

"It shouldn't. I'm pretty sure I know who did it, and I'm pretty sure I can't prove it."

"But you'll try," Susan said.

"One last time," I said.

"Then you'll come home."

"Yes."

There was silence on the phone line for awhile.

When Susan spoke her voice had deepened somehow and become richer.

"And what's the second thing you'll want when you get here?" she said.

I was quiet for awhile lying on the bed, looking up at the un-accommodating ceiling of the house where I had spent too much time already.

"There is no second thing," I said.

"I know. . . . My patient is here. . . . I love you. . . . I have to go."

"I love you too," I said. "I'll be home soon."

"Is Hawk still with you?"

"Yes."

"Good," she said and hung up.

chapter
64

I CALLED MARY LOU to make sure she'd be home. When I pulled the Explorer up in front of Mary Lou Buckman's place, Dean Walker's patrol car was parked in the driveway.

"Both the usual suspects," I said to Hawk.

We got out and started up the walk. The horses in her corral stood at the fence, staring at us silently. The front door opened before I reached it.

"What the hell do you want?" Dean Walker said.

I kept on toward the door.

"We need to talk," I said. "You and me and Mary Lou."

"What's he doing here?" Walker said, looking at Hawk.

"He's here to listen to us talk," I said.

I thought Walker was going to slam the door on us. I believe he thought so too, but changed his mind and stepped aside and we went in. The yellow Lab I'd met before rushed up and began o lap my hand. I scratched her under the chin. Mary Lou was itting on the couch. She was wearing blue shorts this time, and a white tank top. The effect was just as good.

"I can't be alone with you," she said. "I called Chief Walker he minute I knew you were coming."

"Good to find a cop when you need one," I said.

Hawk stopped inside the doorway and leaned on the wall. He ooked bored and amused at the same time.

"What do you want, Spenser?"

I sat on the arm of the couch, at the other end from Mary Lou. Walker remained standing. The Lab came and put her head on my thigh. I patted her. I felt kind of old. I missed Pearl. I wanted o go home.

"Here's what I think," I said. "I think that one day, Mary Lou and Steve were wandering around in the hills around here and found water. I don't know how. Mary Lou's a water resource geologist, maybe she found a spring that was suggestive. Maybe they did some covert drilling. Maybe they looked at surveys and rock formations. I don't know how you find water. But she did and one way or another she figured out that there was a whole new water source. She or Steve or both of them saw what that could mean."

Except for the Lab who was wagging her tail, no one moved. With the heat packed in around the house, there was a kind of timelessness in the cool interior.

"But they didn't know quite how to exploit it, so they went to J. George Taylor, the real estate specialist in the region. He must have liked it 'cause he attracted some investors. Luther Barnes, the mayor, Henry Brown, some others, and they started buying up land."

"Say that's true," Walker said, "which it's not. But say it was. So what? There's no crime there."

"Not yet," I said. "But somebody, along the line, got to thinking that if they could drive the prices down, they could make a much bigger killing much quicker."

Walker said nothing. Mary Lou was motionless on the couch, her knees up, hugging them.

"So they took it to a guy who would know how to do things like that and had the wherewithal to do it."

"And that would be?" Walker said.

"Morris Tannenbaum," I said. "He likes the deal. He sends The Preacher out to organize the Dell and harass the town until people get rid of their homes at fire-sale prices."

"And you can prove all this," Walker said.

"Hell no," I said. "Some of it I can prove, maybe. Some of it I'll probably never know. Some of it I'm making up as I go."

"It sounds that way."

"Sure. It's a harebrained scheme," I said. "But Tannenbaum had his reasons. And everything was going pretty good except that Steve was shooting off his mouth."

"And Tannenbaum killed him?" Walker said.

I took the transcript of the FBI bug from my back pocket and unfolded it and handed it to Walker. He read it slowly, his face showing nothing. Then he handed it to Mary Lou. As she read it she began to blush. By the time she finished her face was very red.

"That's a nasty lie," she said. "Someone has made that up."

She looked at Walker.

"Darling. I never . . ."

"Morris Tannenbaum?" Walker said.

He shook his head, like a horse with a fly in his ear.

"You fucked Morris Tannenbaum?" he said.

"Darling, I swear . . ."

Walker's chest was heaving. The lines at the corners of his mouth were deep.

"What I don't know is whether Mary Lou killed Steve herself, or had Ratliff do it."

Mary Lou hunched forward over her knees and put her hands over her ears and closed her eyes.

"No," she said. "No, no, no, no, no, no."

I felt bad for Walker. He looked like he was struggling to stand. His eyes were reddened and his nostrils seemed to have flared.

"And I don't know if she killed Ratliff, or had you do it," I said.

Mary Lou uncoiled from the couch and stood and pressed herself against Walker.

"I can't stand this, Dean. Please, I can't stand this. Take me away. We'll go away."

Walker's arms were at his side. He was trembling. I could hear his breath heaving in and out. The Lab had stopped wagging her tail and was pressing in against my leg. Leaning on the wall, Hawk looked as if he might doze off. Mary Lou pressed her face into the angle of Walker's neck and shoulder. She had her arms hard around him.

"Please, darling, please. We'll go away. We'll start over. Please . . ."

Slowly, Walker's arms left his sides. They seemed to move on their own, as if he had no knowledge of them. His arms went around her and held her as hard as she held him.

"We'll go," he said. "We'll go."

"Walker," I said.

"We're going," he said.

His voice was hoarse.

"Walker, she killed her husband or had him killed. She killed Ratliff or had him killed. She used her husband. She used Ratliff. She used Tannenbaum. She's using you."

"You can't stop us," Walker said.

With his arms still around her, he turned toward the door. He was wearing a gun, but he made no move for it.

"You will never be able to trust her," I said.

They walked to the door. Mary Lou was still sobbing. The dog left my leg and went after her. Mary Lou put a hand down and took the dog's collar. Hawk looked at me. I shook my head. Walker, Mary Lou and the dog went out her front door and it closed behind them. I didn't move. Hawk didn't move. Outside we could hear Walker's car start up and pull out of the driveway.

"She probably killed several people," Hawk said.

"Or had it done," I said.

"Same thing."

"I know."

"You letting her walk," Hawk said.

"No," I said. "I'm letting him walk."

We were quiet. The house was quiet. I could still smell the hint of her cologne in the cool interior.

"Maybe I'm sentimental," I said.

"Maybe," Hawk said.